BATTLE
BEYOND EARTH
INSURRECTION

NICK S.THOMAS

First published in the United Kingdom in 2015
by Swordworks Books.

ISBN 978-1-911092-43-8

Typeset by Swordworks Books
Printed and bound in the UK & US
A catalogue record of this book is available
from the British Library

Cover design by Swordworks Books
www.swordworks.co.uk

BATTLE
BEYOND EARTH

INSURRECTION

NICK S.THOMAS

PROLOGUE

It is the early days of the 26th century, and Colonel Mitch Taylor is an anachronistic war veteran desperately trying to survive a new war that he never could have imagined. He is a 22nd century war hero brought back in the Alliance's greatest hour of need.

The Krys invasions of Earth have long been forgotten by all but the few elders who lived through them, and the Aranui, whose life span far exceeds any other known life form. Their two races, with the Humans had lived in peace for hundreds of years, alongside the newly discovered Cholan Empire.

That was until a terrifying new threat emerged, an enemy from the past, an alien race that almost brought an end to all other known life in the universe. The Morohta, a highly advanced matriarchal society led by the infamous

Bolormaa, and an undefeated scourge. With their fleets cutting a path through the Alliance, and encountering little effective resistance, it soon became apparent the Alliance could not hold out against this powerful and ancient enemy.

In response, Taylor accompanied a fleet to the Morohta navigational hub in an attempt to block the enemy's travel to Alliance territory and buy them some much-needed time. The mission was a success; despite the high price paid in lives and ships. The Morohta were cut off for as much as a year, time that was desperately needed to fend off their next campaign.

The Alliance had suffered badly at the hands of Bolormaa's fleets, but no more so than the Cholan Empire; who through desperation and a will to survive, turned their backs on the Alliance in their greatest moment of need, a fact Taylor would seemingly never forgive them. Knowing this, the Cholan fleet arrives to launch a pre-emptive strike against the Alliance and win the war in the name of the Morohta. President Isaacs, leader of the Alliance, has been given a one-hour ultimatum to surrender to the Cholan Admiral Eme, commander of the most powerful flagship of the Alliance.

Was the mission to Morohta space all for nothing? Will the Alliance destroy itself even before the ancient enemy can return to finish the job they started? The future of the Alliance and free peoples now hangs in the balance, and there is just one hour left to turn the tide.

.

CHAPTER ONE

The bridge was silent. President Isaacs was grey in the face and staring at the screen before him with an utterly blank expression. Many of the officers around Taylor were looking at one another in horror and shock. Nobody knew what to do and waited for the President to respond with some solution, but it never came.

"What can we do?" Jones whispered.

"We sure as hell aren't surrendering," replied Taylor rather loudly.

"I don't see any other course of action available to us," replied Cohen.

Taylor shook his head. He couldn't believe they were willing to give up so easily.

"You know the power of the Nakbe, Colonel. If we do not surrender, we will all be lost, and still the Alliance will have to surrender."

Taylor shook his head once again. He ignored the Commander and turned to the President, knowing he had the last word in this grave situation.

"If you surrender to them, then all is lost."

"You would rather us die than lay down arms?" Isaacs asked.

"I didn't say anything about dying. I never throw any lives away needlessly. I intend to fight, and if you will not fight with me, then this war truly is already lost."

"Look at it," added Cohen, "Just look at her for a moment," she said to Taylor, pointing to the mammoth vessel on the screens.

"I don't need to look."

"Look at her!" Cohen insisted.

He was exasperated and desperate.

"Do you know why I don't need to?"

Cohen shook her head as the President replied, "Go on, Colonel."

"I don't need to look because I don't need to know what horrors we face, for I have faced more than I care to remember. Never tell me the odds. If I had listened to the odds, I would not be here before you today. In fact, you probably wouldn't even be alive to tell me them. I have faced world-ending ships and creatures that want to tear me apart. Are they terrifying? Yes. But it is our job to stand up and fight those terrors. That is what we do!"

"All just words," replied Cohen, "Sentiment and dreams that you cannot hope to fulfil. This ends in death or surrender, which will you have Mr President?"

"What will happen if we surrender?" asked Isaacs.

Taylor looked to Irala as the only source of information in the room.

"Those who surrendered to the Morohta were never seen again," he replied solemnly.

"But we would not be surrendering to the Morohta, but to the Cholan Empire."

"Their puppets," Jafar added.

"What do you think Lord Jafar?"

Jafar grunted before responding to the President.

"If you surrender now, everything is over; the Alliance, our freedom, and probably our lives, soon enough. I will not surrender, and if you do, then this Alliance is over."

Taylor smiled in response. It was the strong backbone and fighting spirit he had always come to expect from his old friend.

"You would fight and condemn us all?" Cohen asked.

Jafar simply nodded in return and refused to be drawn into an argument. He looked around, noting Taylor had stepped up to the display screens and was studying the images of the Nakbe. It angered Cohen, after the Colonel had refused to do just that when she had asked him to do so.

"There are no weaknesses. You cannot take on that

Capitol ship, not now. Look at our fleet," she said, pointing to the dispersed mix of ships, many of which were still undergoing repairs.

"Get me aboard that ship, and I will bring a stop to this."

Taylor looked down at his console to look at the time they had left.

"Board her? Have you lost your mind?"

"Fifty-five minutes, that is all the time we have left. Might well be the last fifty-five minutes of our lives, so let's make them count."

Cohen turned away from him and rushed back up to the President.

"Sir, I must ask that you bring a stop to this. The Colonel is endangering all our lives."

"You do not command this fleet," added Sarik. He had been lurking in the background. He walked right past Cohen and stopped before Taylor.

"What can we do?"

"Get me and my team aboard that ship, and we will shut her down. The rest of them are your problem."

"Your Immortals? How many of you? Twenty men? What can you do with twenty men?"

Taylor turned furiously to Cohen and grabbed her by the collar. She froze and looked terrified.

"We've been through plenty together already, Commander. I have a lot of respect for you, and you have come through for me in the past. Don't fail me now. We need you to be strong. I need the Commander of the Guam that saw us through the battles of yesterday. You may not like this situation, but it is beyond our control. All we can do is stand up and fight, and keep fighting. Will you stand with me?"

Cohen looked to the President, and he simply nodded.

"Okay...okay."

"Fifty-two minutes," replied Taylor, "That is all we have."

"Then let's do this right," replied Cohen.

He let go of the Commander and turned to address all on the bridge.

"Who can get me and my team aboard that ship in the next thirty minutes?"

"Any ship movement will be seen as a threat," Irala said.

"And you think they will fire on us?"

"You saw the Admiral, Mr President. They are desperate, and desperate men do desperate things," replied Jafar.

"No shit," Taylor said, thinking about the mission they were about to embark upon.

"So how are we going to do this?"

"Commander, do we have any vessels that can approach without being detected?"

Before she could answer he turned to Irala, remembering the cloaking technology some of their vessels used.

"My shuttle can get you close, but not close enough.

Even the best technology we have will still be detected by the Nakbe's systems once she is within a two hundred metres."

"Okay, that's a start. We just have to make it those extra few metres..."

He looked to Jones who was already shaking his head.

"No, no, no, no. No way we can jump it!"

"Why not? The suits can take it. We've got boosters for adjustments. Tell me one good reason why we can't."

"Because it's crazy."

"Come up with a better plan in the next two minutes, and we'll go for it. Gear up, and meet me at Irala's shuttle. Alita, have my kit ready for me."

Both of them nodded in agreement and quickly left.

"With the Nakbe taken out of this fight, can you handle what's left, Sarik?"

"It is a large fleet," he replied.

"But they are a weak race," added Jafar, "They will soon turn tail when pushed."

"Morale, that is their weakness? You are telling me they have no stomach for a fight? No staying power?"

"They do not."

Taylor looked to the centre of the Cholan fleet. Two identical heavy cruisers flanked the Nakbe. After the flagship, they were by far the largest vessels in the fleet.

"Then when you get my signal, you target those two, and only those two."

"But the rest of the fleet, the support craft, fighters, they'll tear us apart."

"Not if you break their will, Commander."

Jafar smiled at the prospect.

"Keep them busy. Arrange for the surrender on neutral ground aboard a shuttle far from here, enough to keep them distracted."

"You want to use me as bait?"

"No, Mr President, you stay put, but root all messages through your shuttle that will head out to those coordinates. Have a few ships join the shuttle, too. Make it look good and convincing. We want all their attention on that."

"And you think this will work?"

Taylor shrugged.

"As much as we can ever know anything. With the three most powerful vessels in the fleet destroyed or disabled, the rest will be terrified. We don't need to destroy this fleet; we just need to make them run."

He turned to leave when Cohen yelled out.

"What will your signal be?"

"You'll know it when you see it."

He rushed out and sprinted for the docking bays. The shuttle was loaded and engines already running as he dashed aboard. Fifteen of his Immortals were inside, all that could fit. Alita was at the door with his equipment. He pulled on his suit as they lifted off.

"Everyone know what the plan is?"

"Kill the bad guys?" asked Antos in a comic tone.

"Fucking ey," replied Taylor.

He took his seat as he pulled on his helmet and made the last adjustments to his equipment. He released the lower shroud that locked onto the suit, sealing all but his visor that was still retracted.

"Think this can be done?"

"Wouldn't be going if I didn't believe it could, Alita," he replied confidently.

"Sure you're not just a dreamer?"

Taylor smiled at Jones.

"Yeah, maybe. But I'm not dead yet."

"You've come pretty close enough times," she joked.

"Close? Who cares about close?"

Jones shrugged at his recklessness, but it was also warming to know he was unwavering and confident.

"These Cholans, are they really as pathetic as they look? Look like school kids that could be snapped between our fingers," said Taylor.

"They are physically weak, but their technology is formidable. However, they have almost no capacity or stomach for close in fighting. The Cholans stay at a distance and fight at a distance."

"That's what I like to hear," Taylor replied, checking his Assegai to make sure it was secure and ready to go.

"You got a plan here?"

"Funnily enough, Jones, yes. You know the best way to

disable a ship?"

"Power and command?"

Taylor looked impressed.

"I've studied your exploits well enough to know how you would do it."

"Kiss ass," replied Alita.

Had it been anyone else, he'd have taken offence, but Jones smiled at her jibe.

"He's right, though. We take down the power, and we seize the bridge, simultaneously. Either target will result in success. If both come through, we gain control of the ship."

"And that is doable with just fifteen of us?"

"With the element of surprise, and some balls of solid steel, yeah," he replied with a smile, "Jones, take seven, your job is to get to the engines. You hear any weapon systems start firing or engines ignite without hearing from me first, you take the whole fucking thing offline, you hear?"

"Right."

"Alita, you're with me."

He shook his head, remembering the betrayal they had faced from the Cholans when they needed them most.

"I can't wait to get my hands on that bastard Eme. I just want to get a grip on his throat and snap his goddamn spine."

"You know they could be our allies yet, if we can get

them back on side? No need to burn all our bridges."

Taylor shook his head.

"We were betrayed once, never again," he said with spite and anger.

Ten minutes went past as they closed in on the Cholan vessel. There were no windows in the hull of the shuttle, not even in the cockpit. It was piloted by one of the Guardians, who finally spoke to them. It was Irala who was clearly in direct charge of the formidable avatar.

"You remember the layout of the Nakbe?"

Taylor and Jones both nodded. "Well enough," Taylor answered.

"This is as far as I can take you, good luck."

"From now on, as far as the comms are concerned, you talk as if we're a maintenance crew aboard one of those crippled ships out there. Anyone who intercepts our signals won't give it a second thought. Remember that, okay?"

They all nodded in agreement. Taylor hit the switch that lowered his visor, and it locked down under his chin. It was so close fitting his nose was almost touching the Perspex. The overlapping plates were in direct contact with his neck, and he felt them dig in slightly as he moved his neck from side to side. It was a claustrophobic, but he appreciated the dexterity and slimline design. He checked around to see that everyone was ready, but Irala had already done so, and the cabin began to depressurise. He felt the weightlessness, but his boots soon detected the shift and clamped down onto the floor to hold him in place.

He took a step forward to the door and marvelled at the horror before him. The imposing enemy vessel filled their view, and he could not help but feel exposed. He expected to be hit by a hail of gunfire at any moment.

"Would be a nice sight... if they weren't, you know, the enemy," stated Jones.

Taylor sighed.

"What's up?" Alita asked.

"Why, oh why, is it always me? Always me volunteering to get my head blown off?"

"Because nobody else ever does."

He turned to see that she was not being sarcastic as he would be. She said it with a sense of pride, and that instantly made him feel more confident about the whole situation. He looked down at the console on his arm. Twenty-five minutes left. He reached around for his suppressor and locked it onto the barrel shroud of his rifle; the others followed suit.

"Remember, only short bursts or the baffles will be fried," added Jones.

"Yep, can't waste any more time. You good to go?" asked Taylor.

He nodded, gritting his teeth as he looked at the monstrous vessel they faced. That was enough for Taylor. He pushed off from the doorway, using only a short boost on his suit. It was enough to put him on course. Alita zoomed up beside him with a small amount of forward thrust to match his speed.

"You confident we can make this happen?"

"Of course. Done it enough times before."

"Really?" she asked in doubt, "This big a job?"

"Haven't you read his file? No job is too big."

"Once again, kissing ass, hey, Captain?"

Jones smiled, but could see it settled the rest of them, including Alita.

Taylor couldn't help but feel sentimental. Once again, he was going into combat with a Jones and the woman he loved. Charlie and Eli were always in the back of his mind, and he would give anything to have them back. For a moment he fell into a hazy dreamlike state and imagined it was in fact those two beside him. They might as well have been, for it felt like he had done this hundreds of times before.

"You okay?" a voice asked him.

It sounded like Eli, but he knew it couldn't be. He looked over to see Alita assessing him as they still soared towards the Nakbe. He looked at her for a few seconds in silence before finally snapping out of it, and nodded in response. As he did so, he noticed they were passing an enemy ship of frigate size and one of the support fleet for the Nakbe. They could only hope they would not be spotted passing through space as nothing more than a few small speckles of debris.

They all knew nobody would be crazy enough to attempt such a seemingly futile and dangerous assault, and yet that was exactly why it could work. No one would say it, though. Taylor pointed for Jones to break off and head to the aft of the vessel.

"Let me know when you've got things under control."

The two groups separated. Taylor looked around; it was just the seven of them now.

Seven to take down the most powerful ship in the Alliance.

It brought a smile to his face. It was a challenge allowed him to take his mind away from the greater threat of the Morohta, or the loss he still felt for the ones he had left behind. He activated his boosters and rotated so that he was approaching the hull feet first, using the power to slow pace rapidly. He landed gently on a flat section of the hull, and his boots immediately latched on to hold him in place. The others landed smoothly around him. He sighed in relief that they had made it, and then looked at the time once again. He pressed a button, and it brought up map information of their position in relation to detailed diagrams of the hull.

Taylor led the small group onwards for thirty metres and stopped. The surface was flush and appeared no different to any other armoured section of the hull, but he knew otherwise, as the diagram showed. He pointed to Antos and gave him a thumbs-up to Babacan who was carrying a huge device on his back that weighed more than any man. It was a signal jammer, and the alien responded with a nod. Alita knelt down at the point Taylor had found and pulled out a small module from her equipment. She pressed a few keys, and a previously invisible hatch popped open.

She looked up at him, surprised it had even worked, but Taylor didn't waste any time. He jumped in to find themselves in a decompression room. Alita sealed the door behind them. They were shoulder to shoulder in the confined space with no room to move at all. Babacan was hunched down, for he could not even stand up with the limited headroom. The feeling of weightlessness faded, and Taylor saw his console was reading an oxygen and breathable environment. He released his visor. It unlocked and retracted back into his helmet. It was a relief to have it off his face.

"Damn they really are little fuckers," he joked, looking at the hunched down Babacan and felt his helmet brushing the ceiling. He pointed to the door that would lead into the belly of the vessel.

"Once we go through that door, we do not stop. It doesn't matter what happens, who gets hurt, we find a dozen enemy combatants, or even two hundred. A lot of people are relying on us today. More than any of you can imagine. You thought the mission to destroy the hub was the most important one you had ever undertaken? Forget it, this is all that matters now. So follow me, and don't stop, not for anyone or anything, you got it?"

They didn't need to say a word. He opened the door and stepped out first into a three metre wide corridor. He didn't hesitate or cautiously peer around into the room they were heading. Whatever was out there, it wouldn't change his course of action. He leapt out and moved forward at a steady jog, his rifle held ready to take aim in a split second. Like everything he had ever seen of Cholan decor, it was lavish and garish in every way; an excess and decadence Taylor just didn't understand.

There was no sign of clutter in sight, or in fact equipment, personnel, nothing. They were in a corridor that could just as well have led to the entrance of a palace. They had not seen a single exit yet, either.

"What do they even do with all this space?"

"If you wanted to make a statement, wouldn't you want the biggest ship in the Alliance?"

Taylor shook his head, but he knew Alita was right.

"I bet they don't have even have half the crew or marines you would want for this size of vessel," added Alita.

"We can only hope," replied Taylor.

His voice faded out as he noticed a bend up ahead and went on in silence. He took the turn with his rifle still held up ready to fire. As he did, he found two Cholan crewmembers approaching. They appeared unarmed and carried tool boxes in both hands. But he did not hesitate; he double tapped both of them in the centre body and rushed on past. He looked down just for a split second to check they were dead. Alita felt bad for them, but she knew Taylor had no choice.

Taylor checked the map displayed on his console for just a second as they reached an intersection, and he veered off towards the bridge. They came face to face with six Cholan marines. They were armed with carbines and wore body armour over just their torsos and tall ceremonial looking Shako hats on their heads. The hats were lavishly decorated and excessively large in some attempt to make them look bigger and more imposing. But to Taylor they looked like toy soldiers. He opened fired with a three-shot burst at the first of them while still moving forward at a jogging pace.

The powerful rifle rounds hit the marine's weapon and armour, penetrating without any resistance at all. Riddled with bullets, the Cholan dropped lifelessly to the deck. Alita opened fire, and they each cut down another two of the marines, but the last of them managed to bring his carbine to bear and in a panic held the trigger down. An uncontrolled burst of fire landed all around them, and Taylor felt the impact of one of the shots on his abdomen, though his armour easily passed off the impact. Both he and Alita riddled the last marine with bullets, but they knew the cat was out of the bag.

"That's not good," said Taylor. He stopped for just a moment and waited in silence. A seemingly long and painful ten seconds went by as they waited for some kind of response. For a moment they could all hope and believe they had got away with it. That the gunfire had gone unnoticed, but it was not to be. The lights began to strobe and alarms rang out, and they knew the game was up.

"Come on, let's move it!" Taylor yelled.

He leapt into action and ran forward at twice the pace of before, with no care in the world or fear of danger at all. The others could only follow after him in amazement.

"Give it a few minutes, and the whole ship will be shut down," said Alita.

"Then we better haul ass!" Taylor hissed.

He hit a button on his console, and his shield ignited and lit up. He knew stealth was no longer of use, but he didn't have a second to waste removing the suppressor from his rifle. There was a doorway up ahead, and two crewmembers were hastily attempting to close it manually. The electronics had failed, and it had stopped halfway. There were several more Cholans behind them. He fired at the first and hit him with two shots to the head, and he was thrown through the doorway.

The other crewmember ducked back behind the doorway. A few seconds later, his sidearm was thrust through the opening and was firing wildly. Shots ricocheted around them. Amazingly, one managed to strike Taylor's shield immediately in front of his face. He rushed to the doorway and pushed his shield up against the opening and stopped to pull a grenade from his webbing, but Babacan didn't stop. The Krys marine ran into the broken door at full speed. It barely slowed his pace as he smashed through and flattened the Cholan on the other side.

Gunfire rang out as he fired at another, and then swung his rifle around and smashed the barrel onto the next Cholan, crushing his skull with the power of the impact and throwing him into the sidewall. The last two turned and ran, but Taylor fired two shots into each of their backs, and they slumped and slid to a halt. Alita shook her head in dismay. It was like gunning children down. They could do nothing against the armour and strength of their team, and yet it had to be done.

They continued on and found themselves in a broad and unnecessarily high ceiling room. It was the approach to the bridge and adorned with jewels and crystal chandeliers. It appeared more akin to a historic palace than a warship. Over thirty Cholan marines were dug in around an improvised barricade up ahead, almost a hundred metres along the lavish and utterly useless corridor. The others formed up beside Taylor in what would have been a neat line, were it not for Babacan towering over them.

Nobody moved, no weapons fired, and no one spoke a word at either end as each side studied the other. Taylor pressed a key on his console, and a small lens slid down over his one eye, providing a telescopic image. He could see the faces of the Cholan warriors. They were terrified. He pressed another key, and a small microphone lowered from the side of his helmet. As he began to speak, the microphone and tiny speaker elevated his voice so that it echoed down the length of the room for all to hear.

"Lay down your weapons and let us pass! You do not have to die here, and we do not wish to kill you. But if you do not do this, you will die."

He took a deep breath, watching them look at one another. Some seemed ready to accept, but one of the officers shook his head, and that kept the others in line. Taylor was disappointed and both sighed and shrugged at the same time. He opened the ports to the single use charges mounted in his shoulder armour, and the others followed suit.

"Let's do this!"

He fired the charges. They soared the length of the corridor and ignited inside the barricades. They were followed by many more as all of them unloaded. Cholan bodies were thrown out over the barricade as they were hit by the salvo. It went silent, and then all they heard were the faint echoes of the wounded crying out in agony.

"Last chance!" yelled Taylor, "Lay down your weapons!"

The officer peered out from over the barricade, and Taylor saw him taking aim. He raised his shield just in time as a single shot struck the energy shield at chest height.

"That's how it is," he muttered.

He looked either side of him and didn't need to say a word. They all held their shields out in a defensive wall and began to advance, quickly accelerating so that they were almost sprinting towards the enemy. The Cholans opened fire with everything they had. Shots hit the shields and walls around them. Taylor felt one impact on the greave armour on his shin. It was enough to almost take him off balance, but failed to penetrate.

* * *

Jones stopped for just a moment to peer around a corner. He knew they were close to the engine bays now, and they had left only a handful of bodies in their wake. It was clear, except for a single Cholan talking to another via a screen in the wall. He was side on to Jones and had not seen him. He waited ten seconds in hope of the call ending, and to his amazement it did.

"We're in luck," he whispered to himself.

He raised his rifle to take a shot, but hesitated as he heard the Cholan continue to talk. He was still in audio communication with someone else on the ship. Jones knew he could not risk a shot and have the crewman give off any sign of what was afoot. He tried to take aim for a headshot, but the Cholan was constantly moving back and forth, as he accessed some sort of console of controls along the wall. Jones lowered his rifle and drew out his Assegai. He raised his hand to signal for the others to stay put, stepped out into the dimly lit corridor, and crept towards the solitary crewman.

A monotonous and continuous drone from the ship's power sources covered the small noises his feet made, and he soon found himself just two metres away. The Cholan turned as if he might have heard something. Jones froze for a moment, trying to decide whether to pounce or wait. The Cholan went back to his work and continued chatting to someone via his comms. Jones was relieved and just about to continue on when an alarm sounded, and red emergency lighting began to flash.

The Cholan spun around and froze as he found Jones standing before him. Neither made a move for a few seconds as they stared each other down. The Cholan looked terrified by the huge armoured soldier, but then quickly reached for the sidearm on his belt. Jones' instincts cut in, and he leapt forward, driving the Assegai into the man's chest. He cupped his mouth with his left hand so that he could not get a word out. Even though he knew Taylor must have been discovered, there was no need to give away their position, too.

It made him feel a little sick to see the life drain out of the Cholan, but he held firm, and the Cholan collapsed unconscious from the massive blood loss. He let the body drop to the deck and looked back to his team, beckoning for them to join him.

"We're almost there."

"But what about the Colonel?" one of them asked.

"Taylor may have been captured, maybe not, but it doesn't matter either way. We have one mission to do, and we are going to make sure it gets done."

He sheathed his Assegai, lifted up his rifle again, and continued on towards the engines. He looked down at his map to see they were approaching the hub that was the only entry point to engineering. He stopped at the end of the corridor and peered around the bend to see for himself.

Jones gasped. More than twenty Cholan marines lay about the hub, and he could make out two heavy weapon positions at the entrance. Further automated weapons scanned the area, and two small armoured vehicles were posted there, too. They were small vehicles, no taller than a Human, with a small turret atop them. To Jones' eyes they looked like a children's toy version of what he might use, but well armed and armoured, and intended for use in the confines of the ship.

"Guess they prepped for this," he muttered to himself.

Bailey looked around, and her eyes widened at all that stood in their way.

"What are we going to do about that? That is an army," she said in horror.

Jones shook his head as he tried to find an answer, but he was speechless.

CHAPTER TWO

Taylor leapt into the air, and his suit carried him a metre over the barricades and heads of the first rank of Cholans. He landed on one of them and crushed him dead with his bodyweight alone. He was already firing with his rifle as he landed and struck another one dead with two shots to the chest. He spun around and clouted the next with his shield. It flashed as the alien connected with the translucent energy and was thrown three metres, smashing into a sidewall. Its spine snapped as it broke over a support beam.

He felt a burst of rounds hit his back, and he turned quickly and found the Cholan officer standing before him. The man who could have let them lay down their arms and live, but would not. The shots had only just brushed the surface of the Colonel's armour, and he returned two shots of his own that killed the officer instantly.

Finally, the room fell silent, and Taylor looked around for any sign of life. There was none. They had cut through the Cholans with ease. Alita couldn't help but feel it wasn't fair, but she was glad to be alive, and that thought overwhelmed all her concerns. Taylor looked at the door to the bridge and could see a small camera tracking his motion from above.

"Come on, Eme, open the damn door!" he shouted.

The Admiral was suddenly projected before him from a piece of glass attached to the camera.

"Colonel Taylor, you have conducted an illegal and immoral violent action during peaceful negotiations. You have broken the very rules of the Alliance you work for, and now ask me to stand down as the leader of a sovereign nation. No, Colonel, you are ordered to stand down, and surrender alongside the Alliance leaders. For you will soon realise that you have no choice, just as they do. This is your final warning, Colonel."

Taylor smiled as he drew out a large explosive device from his back. He walked right through the projection of Eme and towards the door. Just before he reached it, a hatch opened over the door beside the camera. A large three-barrelled gun extended out and aimed towards him. Taylor responded quickly by grabbing hold of one of the barrels, ripped the gun from its mounts, and threw it down the corridor behind him. He looked back at the projection to see Eme looked horrified.

"You're going to regret ever turning your back on us, you spineless bastard," replied Taylor, as he threw the magnetic device onto the doorway and took a few steps back.

"Now, Admiral, this is your last chance. Open this door and surrender unconditionally, or die by my hand. Either way, the Nakbe is mine."

The projection ended. Taylor waited for ten seconds, all the time Eme needed to give up and open the door, but that never happened. Taylor dropped the magazine from his rifle and slotted in a full one, unclipping the suppressor and lifting his arm to access the controls on his console. He looked back to his team for just a second, and then nodded to give them the go ahead. He pressed a key and the charge blew. It was loud, but far from deafening. The device provided a breach just far enough to force the door from its mounts, and it smashed down to the floor.

Lights flashed and shots flew through the opening. Two of them struck Taylor's shield, but he was not deterred. He advanced with his shield before him and his rifle barrel just reaching around its right side. He fired a burst of suppressing fire; the others advanced relentlessly at his side and rear. The smoke from the breach soon dispersed, and he could see one Cholan already dead.

They finished the last few who opposed them. Several of the crew had already laid down weapons, the rest were huddled behind their stations in fear of Taylor and his people.

"Where are you, Eme? Show yourself!" Taylor ordered.

He looked around to every corner of the bridge. At last the Admiral stood up from behind the navigation station. He still seemed confident and defiant, qualities not shared by any of his crew. He brought up a display screen showing the jump gateway, and they could hear the engines of the vast vessel powering up.

"The course is already set, the future already written. We will soon be back in Cholan space, and you will have no choice but to surrender," he said.

Taylor smiled as he pressed a button and opened a comms channel.

"Jones, cut it."

A few seconds later the engine noise faded away, and several warning lights flashed on consoles around the bridge.

"You're not going anywhere," Taylor said, smiling.

"Several Cholan vessels are preparing to fire."

Taylor turned to see Alita was looking at the Admiral's own war table. The entire formation was projected before, it with the manoeuvre and action of every vessel in the fleet.

"You are already too late," said Eme.

The two heavy cruisers opened fire on the Alliance space station, and the badly damaged fleet that had returned there. They were the crews that had seen Taylor's mission to success, and it made him feel sick to know those who were supposed to be their allies were now killing them.

"Call them off!"

But Eme shook his head. "I will not."

Taylor rushed forward, grabbed the little alien by his collar, and hauled him over to the console where Alita watched the battle erupt. The table displayed every ship in live 3D, including the gunfire being exchanged. He drew his sidearm and put it to Eme's head.

"Call them off now!" he screamed.

The Admiral seemed oddly calm and shook his head once again.

Taylor sighed, knowing it would get them nowhere, and he didn't want to be seen as the villain by the Admiral's crew. He smacked the alien over the head with the butt of his pistol and knocked him unconscious. He looked back to the display. Volleys from both of the heavy cruisers flanking the Nakbe were pounding the station. They had closed towards the Alliance fleet to shield the Nakbe. Three Human vessels had already been destroyed, and Jafar's own ship was burning.

"What do we do?" Alita asked desperately.

Taylor thought for just a few seconds, "Can you get control of the weapon systems?"

Alita looked stunned and couldn't respond.

"Can you or not?"

"I...I can try."

"Then do it. Get me the biggest gun this thing has got. What everyone keeps raving about; let's put it to good use."

He watched in horror as the two fleets slugged it out and tore each other apart. Hundreds of fighters battled it out between them. The station was giving as good at it got, but it was close to crippled now.

"We can't put the engines online," said Alita, "The course cannot be altered, not anytime soon, but we need to get the nose around and in line."

"We can use the docking bay thrusters for fine adjustment," said Babacan.

Taylor looked at him surprised, but nodded in agreement for him to go ahead.

"You know the moment we fire one shot they will be on to us, and we're dead in the water," replied Alita.

"But they won't know that. Send enough of a shockwave through these bastards, and they won't stand."

Babacan went at the controls as if he knew what he was doing, and that surprised Taylor even further, but he didn't question it.

"Get us in line with that heavy cruiser and prepare to fire," said Taylor. He pointed to one of the two identical craft that was off their bow to the starboard side.

"Are you going to give them chance to surrender?" Alita asked.

Taylor shook his head.

"You know nobody aboard will survive?"

Taylor nodded.

"And their loss will save many more lives, on both sides," he replied.

She didn't question him any further, but she still felt awful for it. She began powering up the Nakbe's monstrous Goliath cannon. They could feel the entire ship pulse and reverberate as masses of power surged through the vessel. They were banking ever so slowly now and almost in line with the aft of one of the heavy cruisers. Babacan put down a little power to the starboard thrusters and brought them to a halt once more, in plain sight of the engines of their target.

"Fire when ready," said Taylor.

Alita could see there were just a few seconds left until it reached full power. She looked into his eyes, pleading with him without saying a word, but she could already tell he would have none of it.

"Do it."

She closed her eyes and pressed the fire button. A huge burst of energy soared from the Nakbe and hit the powerful heavy cruiser. The impact passed through the ship as if meeting no resistance at all. Explosions burst out all over the hull. The ship was torn into five sections, with thousands more pieces of debris and bodies thrown out into space.

They looked on solemnly for a moment as Alita finally opened her eyes. She wouldn't cry even though she wanted to. The battle came to a standstill; almost every ship and fighter stopped shooting. They were all looking at the devastation between the two fleets. Taylor turned to the most senior Cholan officer still alive, a female Lieutenant. She was trembling.

"Get me a channel to the Cholan fleet."

She didn't respond.

"Now," he replied in a firm voice.

She snapped into action and pushed a few buttons. He took his helmet off and prepared to make a speech he'd had no time to prepare for.

"You are live to the whole fleet," she said begrudgingly.

He hadn't expected for it to be so quick, but after a few seconds he began to address the fleets.

"This is Colonel Mitch Taylor. I have seized the Nakbe in the name of the Alliance. I have no qualms in turning the powerful weapons of this vessel on any ship refusing to accept a ceasefire and offer immediate surrender. Your people..."

As he spoke, Admiral Eme regained consciousness without anyone noticing him in the corner where he had fallen. He drew out his sidearm and took aim at Taylor. His sight was blurred, and he was jaded from the strike, but he squeezed the trigger. A single shot struck Taylor in the neck and passed right through. Taylor staggered forward as he cupped his neck and blood gushed from it. Eme was on his feet before anyone could respond and leapt into view of the camera.

"Do not surrender! Fight for your lives!" he screamed.

Taylor spun around and rushed at Eme with thunderous intent. He had taken pity and let the Admiral live, despite despising him for what he had done. Now he regretted it. Eme lifted his pistol in self-defence, but as he fired, Taylor ducked under and took hold of the Admiral's arm. Two shots rang out and found nothing but the wall of the bridge. Taylor kicked Eme in the stomach, and then drove another kick into his left knee so that the Cholan crumpled and bowed before him. He grabbed hold of the pistol, still in Eme's hand, and turned it to the back of his head.

Eme was powerless to resist the strength of Taylor, even had he not been in his powered suit. The gun barrel reached the back of Eme's head, and Taylor forced his finger over Eme's on the trigger. Blood spewed out over the deck of the bridge. Taylor let go of the Admiral, and his body dropped limp before him. He cupped his neck once again. He was still bleeding, but clearly not enough to suggest the windpipe had been pierced. But then he remembered the video feed. He looked up. Everything had been broadcast to the fleet.

His heart sank as he realised the hope of peace had been dashed. Alita rushed to his side and pulled his hand away to look at the wound. She was oblivious to everything else that was unfolding, but he looked to the operations table. A few ships began to move, and then the firing started once again. He shook his head in disbelief.

"What do we do?" Babacan asked.

He looked to Alita. "How long until we can fire again?"

"Your wound, let's sort you first."

"Fuck the wound, it doesn't matter right now. We do our jobs first and foremost, now how long?" he insisted.

"About a minute," she replied solemnly.

"Not good enough, what else do we have to throw at them?"

She shook her head.

"Nothing that can touch a major warship. The power overload of firing that weapon fries the systems for a little while. We've got close defence systems for protection against fighters. That's it."

"Then what do we do?"

Taylor didn't answer Babacan. It was obvious now. All they could do was sit and wait.

"Why haven't they come for us yet?"

"Who?"

"The rest of the crew aboard this vessel."

Taylor shrugged. "Maybe because to get here they'd have to walk over swathes of their own dead, and realise that none of ours are among them."

"He's right. Nobody could stomach that," added Alita.

They could do nothing but watch the rest of the battle unfold. Half of the ships on both sides were disabled or destroyed. Burnt out hulks floated through space, and still the fight went on. The countdown for their weapon systems seemed to take an hour; at least it felt that way. By the time it was finally ready, the entire area was a scrapyard.

"Ready!" Alita said enthusiastically.

But it felt almost too late.

"Fire," whispered Taylor.

The familiar surge overcame the vast ship once again, and the barrel of the Goliath weapon spurt flame and fire and smashed into the second heavy cruiser, blowing it apart just as it had done the first. Taylor slumped back into the Admiral's seat. He knew it was over, but at a great cost.

"They're running!"

He looked up. The remainder of the Cholan fleet were fleeing through the gateway. It shut down, and finally they were left in peace. Taylor looked over several screens to survey the damage. A number of crippled Cholan vessels had been left behind. Many of the Human and Krys vessels looked beaten beyond repair. Two Aranui vessels had been destroyed.

"Get me some comms. Let's see who is left."

A few moments later the comms officer from the station appeared. He was badly cut and bleeding on one side of his face and burnt on the other, but still doing his job. Sparks flew in the background as crews fought a fire behind him.

"What can I do for you, Colonel?" asked the officer, surprisingly calm.

"What's the damage?"

"We have a lot of casualties, hard to calculate the numbers so far. Most of the bridge crew are dead or wounded. The President and Lord Jafar are in medical undergoing treatment."

"How bad are they?"

"I'm sorry, Colonel. I just don't know at this stage."

"And the rest of the fleet?"

The man shrugged.

"I am getting a few reports in, but many have lost comms altogether. I...we....are just dead in the water. I don't know what to do."

"And Commander Cohen?"

"She...is among the dead, I am sorry to say. I am the highest ranking officer currently reporting for duty here."

Taylor shook his head, realising the extent of the damage.

"I need to get back to you, but I'll need a skeleton crew over here to take care of prisoners and wrestle this beast into submission, can you send a team ASAP?"

"I'll do what I can, Sir."

Taylor ended the call.

"What have we done?"

Alita's voice was full of sorrow and regret.

"What have we done? No, what did they do? What did that piece of shit do?" He pointed at the bloody mess of Eme on the deck.

"We didn't ask for this fight, and we sure as hell didn't want it. Divide and conquer, that is exactly what has been done here. We bought ourselves some valuable time to prepare for the coming war, and now we've probably been set back months, maybe even a year."

"A year?" she asked, looking out at the wrecked fleet, "You think we can replace this in a year?"

"Damn right we can, and we will. Because if we can't, it will be the end of us."

"But...this fleet has been built over probably a decade or more."

"Built in a time of peace. Trust me, war time manufacture can work miracles, and miracles are what we need."

"But you don't believe in miracles."

"Not from any God, no, but I believe men and women can make them happen."

She slumped down to the floor and against one of the units. She looked utterly lost.

"How do you keep going? How do you do it? I don't even want to stand right now, can't. I don't want to fight for this anymore. How do we ever keep moving forward?"

Taylor didn't know how to answer, for he wasn't even sure himself.

"Survival instinct is a strong driving force," stated

Babacan.

"That's the best damn answer I have heard yet."

"But do you believe it?" she asked him.

"Do I think life is worth living? When I have those I love around me, yes."

"And when you came into this new life? You had none of that."

"No," he said, thinking back to those miserable days, "And that is why I was weak. We all need something to fight for. None of us does it for fun, or just out of a sense of duty."

"And when you lose everything you care for?"

Taylor shrugged.

"You find something new and keep moving forward. That is the cycle of life. None of us live forever. Or not too many, anyway."

"Are we destined to lead the life that you have? To fight, and fight, and suffer, and lose, and dance with death so often that we may meet with it any day. To live in that state of fear?"

"Fear? No, no. It may be my curse to go on living while others die around me, but I do not live in fear. Not fear of death, anyhow. We all die. To fear death is to fear life."

He knelt down beside her and took her hand in his.

"This is what is worth living for."

* * *

Hours had passed before Taylor and his team were on their return to the station aboard a transport shuttle. There were large porthole windows running the length of the craft, and they could see the devastation of the battle with their own eyes. Most chose to ignore it, but Alita couldn't bring herself to do that. Something hit the fuselage and bounced off, the body of a Human crewmember that floated on past the windows. A few tears came to Alita's eyes, but she tried to hide them.

As they came into land in the docking bays of the station, they watched a constant stream of shuttles bringing in the wounded. Many were being treated or awaiting treatment on the docking bay floor. There was no space left in the medical facilities. The shuttle reached the ground, and they stepped out to find a stream of blood along the dock floor. There was no triumphant return for them. None knew what they had done, and few recognised them. Taylor reached out and grabbed the nearest orderly as he passed.

"The President and Lord Jafar, where are they?"

The man struggled to get free, but Taylor's grip only got firmer.

"That's secure information that I don't have, and you aren't privy to," snapped the man.

He tried to get free, but Taylor's grip was like iron around his upper arm. So tight in fact that it was starting to cut off his blood circulation.

"I am Colonel Mitch Taylor. Both the President and Lord Jafar will want to see me, so please cut the shit and just be helpful."

The man sighed and reluctantly gave in.

"They are being treated at Zone B, at an isolated ward at the rear of the sector."

"Number?"

"It is unclassified, and an emergency facility for just this very thing."

"You let that secret out pretty easy," replied Taylor, smiling as he released his grip.

"Screw you. There are people here that need my assistance. Why don't you cut the macho nonsense and make yourself useful?"

"He just did. He just saved your ass," Alita said.

But the man had no care to wait around and hear her response. He rushed off in a huff.

"Becoming quite the little badass."

"I learnt from the best."

He went on at a brisk pace, pushing his way through the docking bay area and several sectors of the station before eventually reaching the unmarked area the orderly had mentioned in Zone B. Two heavily armed guards stood at the door, and both of them recognised Taylor instantly. They let him pass, and he strode in to find a dozen more marines waiting on guard inside, where he also found

Sarik. His clothing was cut and several bandages covered minor wounds. Stitches held together a deep cut beside his eye.

"How are they?"

"Both your President and Lord Jafar are stable. They will be okay."

Taylor gasped in relief, "Close call."

"Yes, but we lost many more."

"I need to see them."

"With what in mind?"

"We need a strategy put together right now. The Cholans have run with their tails between their legs, but they are still a threat."

"Not anytime soon, though, surely?" Alita asked. She was now beside him.

"I would strike them quickly while they are still weak. Follow me," replied Sarik.

"Attack?" she asked Taylor as they followed the alien, "With what? We are in tatters."

"And to wait and prepare could cost us more later. We have a resolve that the Cholans do not. We have broken their fleet. Now we must break their will."

They stepped through into a medical room where there were just two patients, Isaacs one side and Jafar the other. Human doctors worked on both, with one Krys aiding them. Both of them were awake and checking through statistics. Jafar had a wound in his flank, whereas the

President appeared to have a broken arm and light cuts. Jafar seemed to be in a much worse state, but he was taking it well. Taylor first went to his old friend.

"Tough old bull, aren't you?"

Jafar turned to greet him but winced slightly as a sharp pain ran through his body.

"Still breathing," he replied.

Taylor turned to the President who had not said a word.

"Mr President, what are your intentions?"

Isaacs looked up. "Intentions? Look at us. We barely got through this alive. Can you not give us some peace to recover what we have left, or is your warmongering state of personality that overpowering?"

Taylor couldn't believe what he was hearing but did his utmost to remain calm.

"Sir, the Cholans have already shown their intent. While the threat of Bolormaa looms over them, and we appear weak in comparison to the Morohta, they will continue to fight us."

"Isn't this much death and destruction enough for you, Colonel? They won't be back anytime soon."

"They will," a voice said from behind Taylor.

He turned to see Irala. Even he had not escaped the brutal effects of the battle. His arm had some kind of wound covering made of a metallic foil, and the left side of his face was cut in many small slices like he had been showered with glass. Taylor welcomed his support and let him go on.

"The Cholans may be weak, but so is this Alliance, and they know it. They will be back."

The President sighed as if he didn't believe Irala, or at least didn't want to believe him.

"What would you suggest?"

"Go after them, and finish them before they can regroup," Taylor quickly added.

Isaacs laughed. "Go after them? With what?"

"Let me return to Tau Ceti and rally the Krys for this new offensive," groaned Jafar.

He fought to get out of bed and strode over to Taylor. He was clearly still in a great deal of pain. Taylor extended a hand to help prop his friend up. Jafar gladly accepted.

"Go, get the support we so desperately need, but let me follow the Cholan fleet and put a stop to this right now," replied Taylor.

"What can you bring into this?" asked Isaacs, "How many ships, how many soldiers?"

Jafar shrugged.

"You must go to the Barbarlars," said Irala.

Jafar's back straightened at the word and shrugged off Taylor's arm. It was clear the prospect was something alien to him. He looked scared, something Taylor had never seen in his old friend.

"Who the hell are they?" Taylor asked.

Jafar didn't want to answer.

"A powerful force that we will need at our disposal," added Irala.

"It isn't that simple..."

But Taylor interrupted.

"Look, we need all the help we can get. If there is some strong force, and there is any chance we can get them on board, we need them."

Jafar shook his head. His shoulders seemed to slump slightly, and he looked terrified by even the thought of it.

"Who are these Barbarlars?" Isaacs asked.

All eyes were on Jafar. He slowly took a deep breath and replied.

"One of the oldest tribes of the Krycenaeans. They are a strong, but simple people. They have rarely sworn allegiance to any Lord, not even Erdogan, and he was related to them by some long forgotten bloodline."

"Why? I thought he united the Krys?"

Jafar shrugged.

"Mostly. But some beasts cannot be tamed. Few have risked it, for were they to try, they could well seize power over all."

"Do they want it?"

Jafar shrugged once again.

"They do not seek it, but given the chance, I believe they might try. They are a savage and untrustworthy people. We would do well to stay clear of them."

Taylor shook his head.

"Unacceptable. We need all the help we can get, and you are going to find a way to get them on board."

"You have no authority or right to ask me for this. You may be a friend, by I am the leader of my people."

"Clearly not all of them," Taylor snapped.

Jafar was insulted but also shamed by the statement to the extent he did not reply.

"You will find a way because we can't do this alone. I'll handle the Cholans, but you better have the biggest and best army ever seen in our lifetimes, or we're finished before we even had time to get started."

"He's right," Isaacs said, "If there is a sizeable force that can help in the war with the Morohta, we need them."

Jafar begrudgingly agreed with them.

"Then I will go to them, the Barbarlars. But do not be surprised if I do not survive the experience."

Taylor could see he wasn't joking, but it was too important not to take the risk.

"Not that is matters, Bolormaa cannot be stopped," he muttered.

But Taylor would not let such a statement pass without clarification.

"What do you mean?"

Jafar looked to Irala, and Taylor could see something else going on that he wasn't aware of.

"Come on, cut the bullshit. There is something you aren't telling me."

Jafar shrugged and finally confessed.

"We do not know how much truth there is, for none of us can say for sure. Bolormaa is a myth."

"You said she existed."

"Yes, but to what extent? The myth says she cannot be killed, nor her sons."

"What the hell are you talking about?"

Taylor looked to Irala as if expecting some explanation, but it didn't come.

"Lord Jafar speaks the truth, as far as we know it."

"So what, she is invincible?"

Jafar nodded. "The stories say her skin is impenetrable by any weapon known, and that her sons have the same armoured skin that makes them unkillable."

"Yeah, we'll see about that."

"You do not understand me, Colonel. You think Erdogan was a formidable foe? He would have been terrified to have to fight Bolormaa or her spawn."

That shocked Taylor and silenced him.

"Unkillable?" he asked.

"There may be a way, but that is a story for another day," replied Irala.

"That's all I need to know. All right, back to the matter at hand, the Cholans. Those greasy little bastards have slipped between our fingers. We have to put a stop to their meddling. Better still, we need them back on board."

"You would trust them again?"

"I didn't say that, Jafar. I don't care what they do. Enslave them and put them to work, for all I care, but we need manpower. However pathetic they might be individually, they have shown themselves to be formidable in more ways than one. So what will it be, Mr President?"

"I don't know what you want from me, Colonel."

"I want a fleet. I want to take this fight to the Cholans and end it."

The President pressed a few keys, and a large screen projected before them. It showed the fleet in orbit and the wrecks still floating amongst them.

"That is the fleet, what do you expect me to do? I cannot give you what I don't have."

"There are still enough serviceable ships here to get the job done."

"And leave us unprotected? Leave Earth unprotected, too?"

Taylor paced back in forth in frustration, for he knew what had to be done.

"Okay, give me the Guam, and two other vessels. That's all I ask."

"And what would you do with them? Fly to your certain death?"

"Just give me the goddamn ships. It's not much to risk, and you know my history well enough that the odds aren't all that bad."

The President looked to Jafar and Irala for assistance,

but they did not come to his aid.

"All right, the Guam and two frigates. That is all, but you are crazy if you think you can succeed. You'll be back here riddled with bullets in no time, if you make it back at all."

"You let me worry about that."

He stormed out. Glad to have been given something, but angry that it wasn't enough.

Irala was the only one to follow him.

"You believe you can do this?" he asked as they left the room.

His whole team was waiting outside amongst the army of soldiers acting as security, and followed him without a word.

"If you can do one thing for me, then yes."

Irala simply waited for a response.

"Get me there. I need a gateway created on the doorstep of the Cholan homeworld."

"That will be suicide."

"Can you do it for me or not?"

"I can give you a ship, but not a pilot. I will not risk our own in such a fool's errand."

"That's what you think this is?"

"I think you might not be thinking clearly."

Taylor laughed and then stopped; turning to face the alien he had come to call a friend, even if he was forever cold and almost emotionless.

"Just give me the goddamn ship!"

"Okay, but no pilot. I will have a Guardian at the helm, who will follow your orders only."

"Thanks," he sighed, "Why does everything have to be so much hard work?" he muttered to himself, as he strode off with his team following and waiting for some news.

CHAPTER THREE

"Three ships to take on the whole Empire, are you crazy?"

Alita paced back and forth in a fury. It was clear she was mad at him, but it was so cute it made Mitch smile. He lay back in his quarters aboard the ship that had become his de facto home. His little smirk only made her more infuriated. She sighed and continued pacing. He simply rested and enjoyed watching her.

"Surely you have a plan that has some chance of working? Because to me this is sounding like suicide, and as much as life sucks right now, I rather enjoy being alive."

He got to his feet and stopped her in her tracks by locking his arms around her. He kissed her lips, and she instantly melted in his arms and forgot all her worries. She took a deep breath and looked up into his eyes.

"Of course I have a plan. You don't think I am in this

life to lose, do you?"

She shook her head.

"That's right. We're born winners. I couldn't have made it this far if it weren't the case."

"But you don't believe in fate."

He shrugged. "No, but it seems to believe in me."

"When do we leave?"

"Twenty minutes."

She recoiled and thought to question his intentions, but he pulled her in close and she relaxed once again, knowing she had to trust him. She yawned and realised how exhausted she was.

"A little sleep wouldn't go amiss," she said, reaching for the stim container beside the bed. She took two, and her eyes widened as she was instantly brought back to a full awakeness. Though she knew she was on borrowed time.

"Gonna be a hell of a come down after all this."

"Just be glad to be alive when you do," he replied.

She offered him the stims, but he waved them off.

"We all need to be on top form for this."

"Yeah, and I will be," he replied confidently.

He kissed her one last time, then let go and reached for his equipment. They headed out into the corridor and passed through several sectors. Everywhere they went they found crews patching up damage from the battle. It was going to be touch and go. They reached the docking bay to find a hundred marines assembled and his team with them. A shuttle had just put down, and a welcome party from the bridge awaited its occupants. An officer stepped out and was greeted by the second-in-command before pacing right up to Taylor. She was a small woman; more than a head shorter than Taylor and petite build. She was clearly from the Far East and looked young to be taking on command of a major warship.

"Colonel Taylor, I am Captain Song, formerly Captain of the Chungmu," she said as she saluted and then shook his hand.

"Formerly?"

"The Chungmu is very badly damaged from the recent battle, and it is unlikely she will ever see service again. I have been given permanent command of the Guam. I pray you keep us alive long enough for me to get acquainted with the crew."

"Will do, Captain."

"I would address the crew, but I know time is not a luxury we have, so please, continue," she said and pointed for him to take up a position on a raised podium. Several screens projected above them showed the Captains of the other two vessels assigned to them. He recognised neither, but their names were displayed beside them. Captain Pollard of the Curlew and Captain Massri of the Taba. Taylor began to address the modest fleet he had been given.

"In just a few minutes we are going to make a jump

into Cholan space. But we aren't going to fight the enemy fleet or their armies. We have neither the time nor the resources. No, we are going to strike at the heart of the Cholan Empire. We are jumping into orbit of Yaxha, right over the Imperial Palace. We aren't going to fight a battle. We are going to overthrow a king."

It sounded crazy, but the marines couldn't help but feel some excitement at the absurd and daring mission he was outlining.

"This is a bold mission, no doubt, but all I ask is that you follow me. We jump in five minutes, be ready. That'll be all."

Jones dismissed the marines and strode up to him with wide eyes. Taylor couldn't tell if it was from the shock of the plan or the stims.

"Well..." he said.

"What?"

"A coup? We are really going to lead a coup? Against the leader of not just a nation, but an entire race?"

Taylor nodded as if it was nothing at all.

"Well, I can at least say they won't be expecting it."

"Exactly. Fortune favours the bold."

"But only fools rush in," replied Jones.

Taylor smiled.

"Indeed."

Jones looked around and could see only two shuttles and a single other transport.

"How are we even getting onto the ground? We're going to need a lot more craft."

"We don't need any at all."

Jones squinted and frowned, trying to work it out, and then he realised what he was saying.

"No way, even you can't be that crazy?"

But he didn't wait for a response. He already knew the answer.

"Get ready!" Taylor shouted. He then stepped over to a line of ammo crates and began filling his webbing with magazines and grenades.

"How many times have you been here before?"

Taylor looked up at the Lieutenant in surprise as he tried to work out what he meant.

"How many times have you lived through this calm before the storm? The final moments prior to embarking on a mission nobody would dream could work, or that you could ever come back from?"

"More than I care to remember."

"And yet here you stand, defiant and ready to do it all over again."

"It's not like I enjoy it."

"Yes, you do."

Taylor thought about it for a moment. He could feel his pulse rising, and it was true. It was not fear lurking in the depths of his mind, but excitement.

Do I really enjoy war that much?

He thought about it deeply.

I know it's a dreadful thing to believe, but it's also carried me through such terrible times. If I did not get some enjoyment out of it, then I would have gone crazy by now.

Song's voice soon came over the speakers.

"Jumping in sixty seconds. Good luck to you all."

A counter appeared over the main docking bay doors, and the last of the ship's crew were rushing to clear the area. All access doors had been cleared of craft.

"Ever done this before?" Alita asked.

"Not quite like this," replied Taylor.

"That's reassuring," she added sarcastically.

"Jump in five, four, three, two, one."

Taylor's stomach turned as it always did when they passed through a gateway. Moments later they felt the ship jolt heavily as it came into contact with the pull of the Cholan world's atmosphere, which they quickly passed through. They could feel the g-force as they made a rapid descent towards the surface. Within seconds a heavy impact, and then several smaller ones, rocked the ship. They knew it was incoming fire and could hear the guns of the Guam returning fire. All power was being put down now to reduce velocity, and Taylor just prayed the ship could handle it. He had visions of them plummeting into the surface or breaking up at any time. The structure of the vessel groaned under the strain.

"Come on, you old girl, you can do it," he whispered.

"So this is what dropping out of the sky feels like!" Jones called out.

He was smiling, but it was forced, for he was also trembling.

They could feel their stomachs go light, and the extreme deceleration and pressure change made a few throw up onto the deck. Then the docking bay doors began to open as they swept in closer to the surface and finally floated to a standstill.

"Go!" Taylor shouted.

They could already see tracer fire flashing by, and the Curlew relentlessly smashed by dozens of missiles and other gunfire, but she was continuing to lay down fire as the marines aboard leapt from the docking bay doors. Taylor didn't even stop to check the distance on reaching one of the broad doorways. He fired up his shield, took a running jump, and soared out into the open sky. It was a beautiful bright sunny afternoon, blue skies and not a cloud in sight, only overshadowed by the vicious battle that had only just begun.

As he began to freefall, he could see they were fifty metres from the surface. Captain Song had brought them in just as he had asked, and he knew it had been a tall order. The boosters of his armour kicked in, and his descent slowed. A gunshot struck his armour and ricocheted off, narrowly missing his face. He looked down for the source of the fire. A Cholan soldier was in plain view and shooting up at them frantically. He took aim and fired a short burst that killed the alien instantly. A second later he hit the ground and dropped to one knee to survey the scene.

They were on a long and broad stone promenade that led up to a vast palace six floors high. Fifteen-metre columns ran the length of either side of the walkway, each one of them lavishly adorned with gold and jewels. There was a statue atop every single one. Up ahead a dozen Cholan soldiers were rushing to engage them, with almost as many lying dead in between.

The Cholan soldiers wore ceremonial attire, bronze looking breastplates and spiked helmets that made them look anachronistic even to Taylor. He took aim at one of them and fired. As he suspected, the bullets passed right through their armour. It provided no protection at all. He noticed a light flashing on his console. It was an incoming called from the Guam. He hit enter as he fired at another target, and Captain Song's voice came through. Her voice was surprisingly calm, but there was still a sense of urgency in it.

"Colonel, the Cholan fleet is on an intercept course, more than twenty vessels. To the North and East troops are already on course."

"What are you saying, Captain?"

"That we can hold right now, but you've got maybe ten minutes at most before we'll be unable to fend off the incoming tide."

"Got it. Good luck, Captain."

"And to you, Colonel."

As the call ended, he fired another burst and forced several of the enemy to go to ground or duck back behind the cover of the columns. They were still several hundred metres from the Palace entrance. Beyond the rooftop he could see the Taba unloading troops to cut off any escape. The marines were going from column to column and gunning down all they came across. He strode forward down the centre of the walkway, his Immortals at his side.

"Ever been here before, Jones?"

"Nope, always wanted to, but I didn't think it would be in this fashion."

"Yeah, well, not much in life ever pans out how you expect it to."

Jones nodded.

They were striding forward at a steady pace now, and it looked like nothing could stop them. The Cholan rifles barely penetrated any part of their armour, and there were so few of them to stand in their way. But just as Taylor thought they would have an easy time of it, the central section of the palace retracted. They all froze, watching with anticipation and concern.

For a moment Taylor thought it was going to be some kind of escape craft about to zoom out from the palace, but it was not to be.

"Oh, fuck," he said.

A vast twenty metre-wide domed turret raised out from it. A huge double barrel cannon protruded from the crown of the structure, and several lighter weapons were mounted in ball joint swivels. It looked indestructible to their small arms and began to pan and track.

"Run!" Taylor hollered.

They scattered in all directions as the main guns opened fire, and two fiery balls of energy smashed into the ground where they had been standing. They blew several metre wide craters into the surface. Taylor jumped and rolled behind one of the columns as sustained gunfire landed all around him. Two marines from the Guam lay dead from the opening salvo, and another was wounded and trying to crawl for cover. Taylor went to step out to go and help, but a dozen impacts hit the column near him and forced him back into cover. He could only stay and watch helplessly as the wounded woman was riddled with gunfire and finally killed.

The big guns fired again and struck two of the columns. They burst from the impact and instantly killed the three marines huddled behind them. Stone fragments peppered Taylor, and the leg of one of the men landed near him. He looked up above them to see missiles impact on the hull of the Guam as she returned fire at the ground defences. Taylor opened a channel to the bridge. Song was in a far more flustered state than he had last found her.

"Captain, we've got a problem!" he yelled. Gunfire still hammered their position, and he looked around the corner. Cannons were taking aim at where he stood.

"Oh, shit!"

He ran to the edge of the walkway and took a leap over the edge, not even knowing what was there. The impacts struck at his back. He was blasted further forward and felt stonework smashing into him. As he was falling, he realised it was into a huge pond and fountain. He hit the water hard and tumbled from the impact of the blast. It was half a metre deep, and he only came to a standstill when he crashed into the base of the fountain. He quickly shook his head and tried to get his bearings, suddenly remembering the screen and what he was trying to do before he jumped.

"I'm on it," stated Song before he even had time to ask.

He looked up. Three small turrets on the underside of the bow of the Guam stopped firing and swivelled around to acquire the new target. It took just two seconds for them to start firing with a salvo of missiles and heavy guns. Taylor looked back to the turret atop the palace and smiled, as it took hit after hit. Part of the roof caved in, and the carapace of the turret was penetrated, but the bombardment didn't stop. Missiles soared through the gaping hole, and an explosion burst out from inside the structure. Half of the dome was blown clean off.

Jones rushed to the edge to see if Taylor was okay.

"They hit the ammo!"

"That's how you get shit done, Lieutenant!" he replied.

He got back to his feet and was dripping wet. He took a run and jumped back up to the walkway beside Jones. A dozen marines lay dead, but not one of his Immortals had been harmed. The rest of marines looked scared and wary of moving forward. Taylor jumped into a sprint towards the palace entrance without another word. It didn't matter whether they would follow him or not. His Immortals were by his side, and nothing would stop him now.

He glanced back. The rest of the marines were turning to face troops that were arriving at their backs, and he was happy to leave them there to deal with it. They soon reached small arms range of the palace entrance, and two-dozen rifles opened fire on them. They advanced as a shield wall, and gunfire was absorbed over every shield. Taylor felt a shot brush off the side of his helmet just as they reached the doors and smashed into the stonework. They each drew out grenades and tossed them through the nearest windows.

With his back against the wall, he watched a dozen Cholan fighters attack the Guam. Its defence systems blew two out of the sky and kept tracking the others, but it continued to take a beating from the ground.

"She can't last forever," said Jones

"Then let's not waste any more time."

Explosions rang out, and glass smashed out across

the ground around them as the grenades detonated. The power of the blasts blew two Cholan bodies out of the windows. Taylor checked the doors, and despite their size and heft, they weren't built for defence at all. He fired a burst into the centre where the two doors met and locked. He then fired at two of the windows and threw a grenade through each. The second after the explosion, he smashed his way through like a raging bull. The doorways gave way under the power of the impact and swung open, crashing back into the walls as far as they could rotate.

A wounded Cholan tried to reach for his rifle, but Taylor quickly put a single shot into his head. Jones and Babacan rushed in and opened fire at soldiers coming through two doorways ahead of them. A vast and lavish staircase was in the centre of the lobby. It split off and curved back on itself to reach up to the next floor. Several Cholan soldiers rushed in from either side of the base of the stairway and were cut down. Taylor knew they had to head up the stairs.

"Babacan, Hariz, Bailey, on me, rest of you deal with them!"

He went forward, firing at the Cholans still trying to fight their way in. With a single leap, he cleared two steps and was rushing up the tall flight. He took the bend where the stairs went back on itself, but was amazed to find no opposition. He carried on up into a large open room with a domed ceiling. Every inch of the dome was painted with what appeared to be religious art. Sculptures lined the walls, but the centre was empty.

Taylor stopped and looked down at the floor plan map on his console for just a second before choosing which arch to take. He pointed to lead the way and ran into a broad corridor. He froze on finding a Cholan captain and five of his men waiting for them. He almost pulled the trigger out of instinct, but their weapons were on the ground, and they were kneeling down empty handed.

"Please, accept our surrender," said the Captain.

He looked terrified by Taylor.

"Your Emperor, where is he?"

The Captain looked down as if ashamed and not wanting to answer.

"Either you lead us to him, or I'll gun you down right here and now. I cannot spare the people or time to take prisoners who will not cooperate. When this is over, you will have your job once again if you do so. Don't, and you won't survive the day."

The Captain saw he was serious. It was clear he recognised Taylor, and his reputation was achieving exactly what he needed.

"His Excellency, Emperor Kuyok is in the throne room of this palace."

Taylor smirked as if not believing the man. He raised his rifle and took aim at the Captain.

"Where is he really?"

"I assure you, the Emperor would consider it a lowly

thing to abandon his throne in the face of the enemy."

"Then he's a fool."

"Like you ever run from a fight," Alita murmured.

"To fight another day, damn right I have. I'm not a fool."

He carefully studied the Captain and tried to calculate if he was being led into a trap, but somehow he believed him.

"Get up. Lead the way," he said.

They went forward with the Captain and his men as shields. They were led through several large and lavish rooms decorated with weapons and armours thousands of years old. They finally arrived at the five metre tall golden doors of the throne room.

"Can't be this easy," said Alita.

They cautiously went forward, the barrel of Taylor's rifle at the back of the Captain's head. As they approached the vast doors, to their surprise, they parted and slowly opened to allow them in.

"What the hell?" Bailey asked.

"It's a trap," said Alita.

"Maybe."

They stopped and waited. Thirty metres at the far wall they could see the Emperor sitting on his throne as if it were any other day, just as the Captain said he would be. There was absolute silence in the inner sanctum of the palace. Only the distant sound of the heavy weapons of the Guam still bombarding the ground could be heard. Through the doors the only other sign of a life was a single Cholan warrior standing a metre away from the Emperor. He was a bodyguard and dressed in a powered suit not unlike Taylor's.

The Emperor wore the crown of a King and was lavishly clothed in purple and gold. To Taylor he looked like a circus clown, but there was no doubt they were a wealthy people.

"Colonel Mitch Taylor!" a voice called.

It had come from the Emperor, but projected artificially through some hardware. It reverberated round the room and sounded deep and imposing. Taylor smiled.

Well, that might intimidate some people, but to me it is just the sound of a little man in a high tower.

"I'm Taylor!" he yelled back.

His voice carried strongly along the long throne room with no artificial aid at all.

"Step forward, and let us discuss this as friends," the response came.

Taylor couldn't believe what he was hearing. He looked to Alita, and she seemed just as surprised. She was shaking her head to tell him not to do it.

"Call a ceasefire and we'll talk!" he replied.

"Agreed!"

He tapped his console and brought up the Guam once again. Song appeared on the screen and said nothing, waiting for him to speak.

"Cease fire."

"What?" she asked, as if she thought she had heard something crazy.

"Just do it," he replied and opened a channel to all forces.

"This is Taylor. Cease fire and hold your positions!"

They heard the gunfire stop just a few seconds later. He could see Song carefully studying her scanners and looking in amazement.

"Is it over?" she asked.

"Not yet. Anyone fires a single shot, then you return it tenfold, but you do not start the fight, you hear?"

"Yes, Sir," she replied, sighing in relief. She replied with a whisper for just him to hear.

"Colonel, we're not in good shape. I've got multiple breaches, and half our weapon systems are down. Engines are damaged. I am amazed we are even still in the air. If this fight resumes, we will be finished in a matter of minutes."

"Understood. Hold fast."

He ended the communication and pushed past the Cholan Captain.

"Don't do it," pleaded Alita.

"Don't worry. I'll be fine."

"But I do worry, all the time."

He smiled and reached out, brushing his hand across her cheek. It brought her a few seconds of comfort before he broke contact and carried on into the room. He deactivated his shield and advanced with his rifle lowered in one hand to his side. He didn't trust the Cholans one bit, but it was worth some risk to save those he had brought with him. Two metres inside he stopped cautiously. Now he could see more than twenty Cholan officials standing either side of the room, and a number of security guards and officials lurking beside them. He counted twelve that could be a threat, not including the bodyguard next to Kuyok. The Emperor spoke once again.

"What is it you want to achieve here, Colonel Taylor?"

"Do you lead your people?"

"I do."

"Then it was you who gave up on the Alliance, and you who ordered the attack on those who remained within it?"

"I did, but only for the good of my people. You must understand that, and you would have done the same for your people."

Taylor shook his head.

"Then you know nothing. You are a danger to the freedom and survival of the Alliance, and you lead your people into an alliance with the worst scum in the universe. The Morohta are a disease, an infestation, and any one who supports or enables them is no better."

The Emperor could see he was getting nowhere and tapped a control on the armrest of his throne. Taylor heard the doors at his back begin to close. He looked back to Alita.

"No!" she screamed, trying to make it through, but the doors slammed shut as she crashed into them. Huge buttresses swung into place and sealed the room like a vault. Alita looked back to the Cholan Captain with disdain.

"How do we get in?"

He did not respond.

"How!" she shouted at him.

"There is no way."

She looked to Bailey.

"Can we blow our way through?"

Bailey smashed the underside of her fist into the walls and shook her head.

"I've never seen anything like them. We're gonna need more than a few breaching charges to get through this. Bring the Guam's guns to bear and maybe we could put a hole in it, but short of that, we're stuck."

Alita turned to Babacan as if expecting to hear something different, but he had nothing. She spun around and smashed both her arms into the doors. She began to wail.

"Trust in the Colonel. Lord Jafar always did," Babacan added quietly.

"I trust him. I really do, but I also fear for him."

* * *

Taylor looked around the room from one face to another. Most were part of some type of court to the Emperor and officials of all sorts. They looked like yes men to him, and he knew their will could be broken easily, but he was also wary of just how many potential enemies he had been locked in with.

"You have no authority here," Kuyok stated.

He waved towards Taylor, and twelve soldiers stepped out from the sidelines as a barrier between him and Taylor.

"Detain him!" Kuyok ordered.

As they raised their rifles, he raised his left arm, and they stopped. They saw he was holding a grenade. He twisted the priming cap with his thumb and watched them look at one another in a panic. They had no idea how to deal with him.

"You just made a big mistake," replied Taylor.

He tossed the grenade, and it landed at the feet of the soldiers. He leapt off to one side and rolled until he was behind the cover of a pillar. Bullets landed all around him. The explosion rang out, and he looked back; three had been killed by the blast. The others had taken shelter behind similar pillars nearby. The Emperor's bodyguard stood in front of him with a shield similar to Taylor's, but Kuyok refused to move.

"Fool," Taylor muttered.

He looked for another grenade, but there were none left. He knew they were so terrified now in the sealed confines of the throne room that a decoy would be enough. He pulled out the suppressor for his rifle and launched it towards the opposite corner of the room. As they panicked and rushed for cover, he stepped out from the other side of the column and rushed forwards. Two Cholans were in plain sight from where they had sought cover.

Taylor fired two shots at them, and they died instantly. He was on top of their position in seconds when a rifle barrel appeared from behind cover. He didn't even slow down but grabbed hold of the barrel and rushed past, launching the Cholans off their feet and slamming them into the wall behind him. Taylor fired a three-shot burst into the soldiers. They were dead before they even had enough time to reach the floor.

He leapt into the opening between two pillars to find the remaining soldiers had lain down their weapons. The other officials knelt beside them. Taylor couldn't believe they had give up so easily, but he was relieved.

"Fight him!" pleaded the Emperor.

Kuyok's cool demeanour had gone. He kicked out so that a footstool was launched down the few steps leading to his throne, and he was up on his feet beside his bodyguard.

"Fight him, you dogs!"

But they looked up to Taylor as their new master.

"Somebody get that door open, now!" Taylor ordered.

One of the high-ranking officials rushed to the entrance of the room with a soldier in tow. No one else made a move. Taylor watched cautiously, but to his surprise, they did exactly as he had said. They punched in codes to wall-mounted devices either side, and sure enough the doors parted.

His three companions came rushing through and instantly pinned the two Cholans to the inner walls. They froze with shock to see Taylor standing before the dozens who had surrendered to him. He knew all was not done yet but was glad to have someone covering his back. He went forward, and the Cholans separated so that he had a direct path to the throne. As he drew nearer, the bodyguard came down the steps and met him halfway. The Emperor grinned wickedly.

"This is Tuin, the greatest warrior the Cholan Empire has known in seven generations."

Taylor didn't look impressed, but the Emperor seemed confident, which at least made him take the situation a little seriously. Tuin drew out a long and curved single-handed blade that sizzled with fiery energy.

"Don't do it, Mitch. We're so close now," Alita begged him.

But Taylor couldn't help himself. He wasn't sure if he was doing it as a matter of honour or simply for the challenge, but he was already impressed that the Cholan had stood by his Emperor, and was willing to stand against

Taylor when all others had given in. He threw down his rifle and drew out his Assegai. With his powered and armoured suit, the little Cholan came close to the size of Alita without her armour on. Meaning Taylor still stood as a giant in front of him.

"You would die for him?"

Tuin simply nodded.

"Well, okay, then," Taylor replied casually.

"You know you can stop anytime? You don't have to die for that bastard."

But Tuin just stared at him with a blank expression. Taylor couldn't tell if he was being studied or had scared the alien. He raised his shield and took a fighting stance. As he did so, the Cholan rushed forward with such blinding speed it shocked him. Tuin jumped as if he intended to barge Taylor, but instead placed one foot onto his knee and leapt over him into a flip. As he did so, he slashed with his blade. The sword sliced deep into the backplate of Taylor's armour and came close to penetrating. As it drew up towards the back of his head, the tip just slashed lightly into the back of his neck and base of his ear.

Taylor grimaced from the pain as he spun around and swung a little clumsily with his Assegai, but the Cholan was already beyond his reach. Out of the corner of his eye, he noticed Alita raise her rifle and take aim at this new threat.

"Don't you dare!" Taylor yelled angrily.

Alita sighed in despair but lowered her weapon, as she knew Taylor wanted her to. He turned back to Tuin and could see he was being circled now. The confidence of the alien was admirable, and he could see now that it was founded in reality.

"What do you know, a Cholan with balls, backbone, and the skills to put them to use," he said, smiling as he felt blood dripping down his neck and tainting his uniform beneath the suit. Tuin still said nothing and rushed forward again, leaping into the air much like he had before. But Taylor was not going to underestimate the warrior a second time. He took a quick step back and swiped his shield across the Cholan's, which sent him into a spin. As his flank was exposed, he thrust his Assegai forward. But with his immense speed and agility, the Cholan dropped low and parried with his own shield just a split second before impact. Taylor kicked under the shield and launched him three metres across the room. Tuin landed hard, rolled twice, and spun back up onto his feet, ready to come at Taylor once more.

He rushed forward and swung with three fast cuts against Taylor. He parried all of them, but on the last cut the Cholan stopped half way and redirected to the other side. Taylor could not move his shield quick enough to counter the fast deception and had no choice but to parry with his Assegai. The sword connected and cut it in half, slicing through into Taylor's arm. The blade cut deep enough to draw a centimetre into his triceps. Taylor responded by punching forward with his shield. The impact was enough to throw Tuin onto his back, and Taylor quickly went forward to stamp down on his face.

Tuin rolled nimbly out of the way, but before he could raise his sword, he found Taylor's boot stamp down firmly on the blade, pinning it to the floor. The Cholan released his grip and rolled out of the way and back onto his feet. Taylor kicked the blade out of the way as Tuin powered his shield down, and Taylor did the same. Despite the pain and injuries, Mitch was really starting to enjoy himself now, but he was also starting to wish he did not have to kill the Cholan who had shown so much promise.

"Surrender," he said.

Tuin raised his arms into a fighting stance and shook his head to refuse. He came forward with a kick to the inside of Taylor's leg. The Colonel teetered slightly before he returned a powerful straight punch. His reach easily allowed him to strike the Cholan hard. His head snapped to one side slightly, but as Taylor lunged again, Tuin ducked under, punching Taylor to the face and breaking his nose with a precise strike. Blood burst out from both his nostrils and streamed down his face. Taylor staggered back slightly and smiled to reveal his blood soaked teeth.

"Well played," he stated and went forwards.

Taylor knew he had to be smarter and more refined with his actions now. He swung as if he intended a heavy hook, but as Tuin tried to duck under, he struck a kick with his long reach. The alien's hands rose up just in time, but it was not enough. The power knocked him back and stunned him. Taylor leapt forward with a flying punch that struck him in the left eye. The impact seemed to stun Tuin. Taylor followed it with an elbow into his collarbone from above, and he keeled over. He could see Tuin was defeated but could not bring himself to kill the warrior who had fought so valiantly and with such skill.

His fist was held up ready for the final hammer blow. He quickly struck, and Tuin was knocked flat down to the ground. Utterly defeated, and with nothing left to give, he finally nodded in agreement to acknowledge his defeat. Taylor was glad to accept it. They could hear the thunder of footsteps. Jones and several of their Immortals rushed into the room in support, and then stop in amazement to see Taylor's condition and the standoff between him and the Emperor. Jones didn't say a word. He simply nodded to give his support. Taylor looked back at the Kuyok, who for the first time looked truly scared. Taylor's expression towards him was contemptuous.

"Colonel Taylor, we can surely work something out."

Taylor didn't say a word. He quickly drew the pistol from his side and fired a single bullet. It hit the Emperor between the eyes and killed him instantly. His body slumped forward. As he smashed down to the ground, the crown toppled from his head and rolled across the floor, coming to a standstill just a metre in front of Taylor. Jones couldn't believe what he was seeing; the others didn't fully appreciate the severity of the situation. He lowered his rifle and walked up to Taylor. The Colonel simply stood looking at the body of the dead Emperor that he had slain.

"What have you done?"

But to his surprise, it was not remorse Taylor was feeling, only a sense of achievement.

"Completed the mission," he replied confidently.

"Is this really what we came here to do?"

Taylor nodded.

"We came to do whatever was necessary to ensure the Cholans no longer presented a threat, and that they would fight for us," he replied, looking down at Tuin.

"Do you understand that?" he asked the Cholan.

Tuin nodded.

"I understand," he replied sincerely.

"You were willing to lay down your life to protect him, and yet this does not bother you?"

"I did everything I could to fulfil my duty, and I must continue to do the same for my people."

Taylor was impressed. He was the only Cholan he had ever found he could relate to, and as he swept the blood from his nose, realised an opportunity had presented itself.

"I don't want to seize power here. I only want the Alliance to be as strong as it can be. This back and forth, this violence, it ends today, you understand?"

Tuin nodded slowly. Taylor took a few paces forward and reached down to pick up the crown. He studied it for just a moment. It was far heavier than he had expected and could see from the rare jewels that it must be priceless. It was also tarnished with the Emperor's blood. He looked over to Tuin who didn't understand what he was doing.

"I need someone who can be trusted to lead your people. You are the only candidate I am willing to back, want the job?"

Tuin shook his head.

"I cannot. I am not of noble birth."

Taylor smiled, knowing he had the right man. He tossed the crown into the alien's lap. Tuin caught it and almost seemed scared to touch it. He held it up and at a distance. It was clear he had never handled it before. One of the Cholan officials stepped forward in an exasperated fashion.

"Sorry, Colonel, but you cannot do this. We have a strict tradition that must be adhered to, and..."

Taylor swivelled around and glared at the alien, who stopped when he saw the pistol still in his hand.

"You know what I have learned about tradition?"

No one dared say a word and waited for him to continue.

"I learned that it changes in time. Whatever you have been doing, it isn't working, and whether you like it or not, I am here to tell you things are changing."

He stepped over to Tuin and hauled him to his feet.

He took the crown from his hands and placed it on the Cholan's head. Tuin still looked uncomfortable, but Taylor placed a hand on his shoulder and reassured him.

"You are a better man than all these assholes. You've got skill and courage, and that is enough."

He offered out his hand, a gesture Tuin clearly recognised but had never experienced. He took it eventually.

"If you continue to show the courage I saw here today, then I will gladly call you my ally, and my friend. Your people need you. The Alliance needs you. Will you step up and do what needs to be done?"

Tuin looked past Taylor to the Cholan officials. It was clear none of them approved, but he nodded in agreement anyway.

"This won't be easy. There will be many who contest this."

"And you will deal with them. There cannot be another war or another division between us. Together we will fight the Morohta, but divided we will almost certainly fall."

Taylor strode up to the other Cholans and walked up and down the line. He intimidated them, and it was no surprise.

"You will support Tuin as your leader, or you will answer to me."

He looked back to the new Emperor and nodded as if to hand over to him. "Good luck," he added.

With that, Taylor picked up his rifle, turned, and left.

"That's it?" Jones asked, as they passed through the palace doors, "What is to stop them coming at us again?"

Taylor shook his head.

"We can't enslave them. We have done all that we can do. Now they must sort it out amongst themselves. Something tells me Tuin will be a far more formidable leader than they could ever have imagined."

CHAPTER FOUR

Jafar groaned as he lay back into his chair aboard the bridge of the Yavuz. Sarik stepped into the room just in time to see his Lord suffering from the wound that was not yet healed, but he would not ask after him in front of the rest of the crew. Jafar studied the bridge carefully.

"Been a long time since I have been aboard this old warhorse."

His sentimentality amused and confounded Sarik.

"You speak like a Human," he added in a friendly tone. Jafar nodded.

"You should continue to learn everything you can from humanity. For a weak people with just one planet, they defeated every fleet our forebears ever threw at them."

"I do not doubt their strength and ingenuity, but you would be wise to remember your origins if you are to visit the Barbarlars. They are not forgiving, and will only see your Human tendencies as weakness."

Jafar sighed as he thought about the road ahead.

"They will not fight for us."

"Then why are we going?"

"Because however unlikely, we have to try. Taylor showed me that."

"What exactly?"

"To not trust the odds. That often victory can be sought through adversity, no matter how severe or seemingly insurmountable."

"You are becoming philosophical in your old age."

Jafar noticed just a hint of humour in his voice.

"You are not without Human influence either."

Sarik did not respond.

"Plot a course. Let's get this over with," said Jafar.

"Are you sure you do not want to take a larger fleet? One Battleship and two support vessels will do little in the event that the Barbarlars take offense."

Jafar shook his head.

"I will not weaken the Alliance position here, and we cannot risk any more."

"But we are risking you, our leader. What if you were to fall?"

"Life will go on. Set the course, and get us moving."

He looked around to study the vessel. It was almost a hundred years old, and yet still one of the most powerful ships in his fleet. He could see its resilience in the battle with the Cholans only served to show the strength of the Yavuz.

"I am sorry we could not transport you on a more modern warship," added Sarik.

Jafar shook his head.

"The Yavuz is battle proven. Dependable. I'd rather rely on a ship with a proven history than the latest technology and a polished interior."

Sarik barked a few orders, and they were soon going forward towards the jump gate. It powered up, and Jafar knew there could be no turning back.

"Do you believe Colonel Taylor can succeed?" Sarik asked.

"I have no doubt he will. There is not a task that man has set himself to that he has not achieved. One has to wonder if he was sent by a higher power."

"Do you believe he was?"

Jafar shook his head.

"I do not know anymore. Certainly what he has accomplished goes beyond what anyone could ever have believed possible. Maybe he is the Dusmus Kahraman."

He had said it almost as a joke, an off the cuff remark, but Sarik had taken it very differently.

"You cannot believe he is the one?"

Jafar looked around to see the entire bridge crew had heard him and stopped in silence to hear him go on. It was in this moment he began to wonder at the significance of the legend.

"Dusmus Kahraman, the fallen hero," he translated as he thought more deeply at the matter.

"Could it really be? A fallen hero returned to us in our greatest time of need?" asked Sarik.

Jafar didn't believe it, for he never believed the myths and superstitions of his people, and his time with Taylor had only reinforced that position. And yet he saw the rise in the morale of the crew, and that he could use it to his advantage. He rose out of his chair to address them.

"Is Mitch Taylor the Dusmus Kahraman? I cannot know, and neither can you. But each of you should think about everything he has achieved. The legend never stipulated that the Kahraman was one of our own, only that he fought for us, and died for us. This world that was created, this paradise we have lived in since the demise of Erdogan, Taylor created that. It was Taylor who put me on this throne. It was he who enabled our people to live on Earth, who brought peace with the Aranui. Is he the Kahraman? He might as well be."

He was even starting to believe it himself and felt it had captured the imaginations of those around him.

"Taylor has gone to conduct one of the most important missions of the war, and like ours, he had too few resources and too little time. But he would never let that make him believe for a second that he could fail. I know what you think of the Barbarlars, for I think the same. They are a savage people that I would rather never encounter in person. When we arrive at their world, I ask for just two volunteers to come down to the surface with me."

"I will go," Sarik said without hesitation.

Jafar shook his head.

"Anyone but you, my friend. I will not risk any more here than we must. The war may go on without me, but the Alliance needs every strong fighter and ship it can assemble. If I encounter resistance when I meet with the Barbarlars, you will run, and that is an order!"

Sarik's lips were sealed.

"Promise me you will follow that order, even if it may be my last?"

"We swore an oath to you, how can we leave you?"

Jafar took a deep breath.

"Some things are more important than one man."

"And yet you would not say the same about Taylor?"

"But Taylor is no ordinary man. Just do this for me. Do not risk these ships and your lives in any futile attempt. If this is my end, and that is my fate, so be it. I am old. My best years are distant memories. This is your time. Now take us through, and let us do what we can."

He took a seat as they passed through the gateway, and Sarik knelt down beside him so that they might talk more privately.

"You don't believe there is any chance of this working,

do you?"

"No," replied Jafar quickly and quietly.

"Then why go at all?"

"Because that is my duty."

Sarik looked frustrated. Jafar laid a hand on his shoulder.

"You will run if things go badly down there. Trust in Taylor. He is the key to victory, but he cannot do it alone. For it is not what he achieves individually that decides the outcome of a battle or a war, but what he inspires and the success he manifests in others. If I fall, he will support you in taking up my position as the leader of my people. It is my final wish that has been documented and arranged. With him by your side, you will make a great leader."

"Let's not talk like you are already dead."

"Don't think I want to be. I am not going down there to fail. I will, as I have always done, do my utmost to succeed. But we live in difficult times, the most difficult since the demise of Erdogan. I have lived through many wars, and I may yet survive this one yet. As Taylor would say."

They passed through the gateway that returned them to Krys space.

"It will be almost twenty hours before we can reach the Barbarlar sector. You should rest," said Sarik.

Jafar was glad of the suggestion and left the bridge.

Sarik noted the crew were uneasy and restless. None of them wanted to go anywhere near the Barbarlars. Sarik himself thought back to the only encounter he had ever had with them, and it almost cost him his life. But as he rested back in his chair, he began to think of the Dusmus Kahraman myth. He had grown up with tales of Taylor and never once linked the two together. He still didn't believe an alien could represent the myth, and yet it gave him some hope.

The time passed slowly as they travelled to the Barbarlar homeworld. They were nearing a moon outpost when finally they made contact. Two craft were on an intercept course, smaller than the three vessels they had taken with them. Before Sarik could say a word, the door behind him opened and Jafar strode in.

"Will they fire on us?"

Jafar shook his head.

"We do not come in great enough number to pose a major threat. They will see this as exactly what it is."

"And what exactly is that?"

"Diplomacy."

"I am not sure they know that word."

"We are being hailed," said the comms officer.

"Put them through," replied Jafar, "They need to know I am on board."

"Why?" Sarik asked.

It was clear he was more concerned they would be fired upon as a result.

"Because they will understand the severity."

"I do not like this at all," replied Sarik as the screen

displayed one of the Barbarlars. The face shape was recognisable, but black and white face paint and loose deep red and black clothing made him look like something out of their history books. The face was more wrinkled and a little simpler and angrier looking than a typical Krys.

"What is the meaning of this invasion of our space?" he demanded.

Sarik was unimpressed by the man's lack of introduction and rude tone, but he left Jafar to deal with it.

"I am Lord Jafar, leader of the unified Krys worlds. I come in peace and wish to meet with your leaders."

"We have no reason to talk."

"But we do. A threat exists that will come to your world after it is finished with ours. I offer my hand in friendship so that we might fight this threat together."

The alien's face seemed to light up slightly at the prospect of combat, and Jafar knew that was the bait with which to catch the primitive elements of these people.

"Hold your position, and I will take your proposal to my Lord."

Jafar nodded for Sarik to issue the order.

"Reverse thrust, hold position," he added.

The transmission ended abruptly without another word. Had it been anyone else, they would have assumed the signal had been lost, but it was clear that they were abrasive and rude.

"Are we really going to try and make a deal with these

animals?"

"Yes, you won't dissuade me. If there is any way we can make this happen, we must. No matter what it costs."

There was an uncomfortable silence that lasted a few minutes while they waited for a response. Sarik was checking the scanners for any more enemy vessels every few seconds, clearly expecting them to come under attack at any moment.

"Relax, they have no reason to strike at us yet," Jafar finally said to calm everyone's nerves.

"That isn't very reassuring," replied Sarik.

A light suddenly flashed, and the comms officer accepted the call to find them facing the same Barbarlar they had spoken to just moments before.

"You have been granted an audience. Coordinates will be relayed to you shortly. Be warned, any sign of aggression will be taken as an act of war and responded to with force."

The call transmission ended abruptly once more.

"The planet of Erzurum," Jafar stated. They looked at the solitary world before them, "Has any one of you set foot there before?"

There was no response.

"Never before have I seen an inhabited world as hostile and barbaric as this. The Barbarlars are hardened by the fact that only the toughest and most resilient survive. There are more than a dozen predators that would eat any one of us alive. Some of the Krys have even wrestled those into submission and ride them as symbols of their strength and power. They use advanced technology only when they have to. A few ships to monitor the outside world."

"If they are so formidable and yet primitive, why did Erdogan not force them into submission when he had the chance?"

Jafar nodded in agreement, for it was a good question.

"Some legends say the Barbarlars are the oldest of our people, and not one Krys Lord would spill their blood in any way that would be considered dishonourable, or risk angering millions of our people. The only way to deal with the Barbarlars is to get them onside as allies, or to beat them into submission using your bare hands."

"Then we are forced to live according to their barbaric ways?"

Jafar nodded again.

"We will do whatever must be done."

"I have the coordinates for you, Sir."

"Remember to do as I ordered. If you do not hear for me in twenty-four hours, or are fired upon, you leave. Those orders must be followed, and Sarik, if you will not follow them, I fully expect every member of this crew to overrule you."

"Understood," he replied solemnly.

"My volunteers?"

"More than half the crew have come forward, but I have selected two of the very best," replied Sarik.

"Very well."

He left the bridge without another word. He was still wearing the same slimline armoured suit he wore in his everyday duties. He knew it would be a mistake to arrive with any kind of pomp and ceremony, for it would have the exact opposite effect as would be intended with any other situation. Many of the crew he passed on his way to the dock stopped and nodded their heads in respect and appreciation. They acted as if he was walking to his death, and to some degree he felt that, too.

But then he thought, *what would Taylor do?*

And he righted his back and walked a little taller.

Taylor would tell me to not fear death. He always said the same to those that followed him. It is time for me to live by his words.

The two soldiers awaited him. They had been selected from Sarik's personal elite unit. They each carried pulse carbines, a brace of pistols, and retractable powered glaives on their backs. It was the signature equipment of those he had trained personally.

"Your names?" he asked them.

"Boz and Gur," came the responses.

"Neither of you fires without my order. Do not lay a hand on any of them or even look at them in a threatening manner. I do not care what happens, but while I am still breathing, you will not fire without my order, understood?"

They acknowledged in agreement as he carried on into a shuttle that was waiting for them. Boz took the pilot's controls. Jafar took a seat and watched the door close behind him, wondering if it were the last time he would see his friend Sarik. They lifted off, and he looked to Gur sitting opposite him. They did not exhibit an ounce of fear. While he respected them for that, he knew it was merely through inexperience. No one would ever go to Erzurum and not be scared.

"Have you ever met a Barbarlar?" he asked.

Gur shook his head.

"Do not underestimate them. They may look like simple creatures, and in some respects they are, but they are also savage beyond belief. Many of them would tear you apart just for their own entertainment."

Gur nodded.

"You are allowed to speak."

He nodded once more, and Jafar assumed he simply had nothing to say. He was a loyal fighting machine and little more.

"I may be leading us to our deaths, and I am sorry for that."

"You are our Lord, and we would follow you anywhere you asked," replied Boz.

"Maybe you should not. A leader is not always right or just. I stand before you now because I did not follow my Lord. The society we have today was created through something very different, and it certainly was not blind loyalty."

"This loyalty is not blind," Gur finally said.

Jafar appreciated the sentiment, but there seemed little else to say. They were soon breaking into the atmosphere of Erzurum. They were no signs of cities or modern infrastructures. For kilometres in every direction there was only thick jungle like foliage and craggy rock outcrops. The foliage was of a deep red and darker green. It seemed to give a tint to the world like a deep blood red sunset back on Earth. A single small fighter zipped past them, and another soon came alongside to escort them down to the surface. A roar sounded from the other side of the craft, and a large winged beast flew into view.

A Barbarlar rode the monster with its ten-metre wingspan. Its dark yellow and brown striped scales looked like they could stave off the most robust of weapons. Its stubby and strong snout had gnarly and vicious looking teeth. Steel chains were lashed around its mouth and throat as a means of control, giving the impression it would rather eat you than have you ride it, and yet they did.

"They are called Ejdars," stated Jafar, "According to legend, they were common across all our people at one time, thousands of years ago."

"This really is our homeland? This is where we came from?" Gur asked.

Jafar shrugged. "I really don't know anymore, but they

believe it, and that is all that matters right now."

"What can these primitive creatures possibly contribute to our fight?"

Jafar was amused that Gur didn't see it.

"This planet is occupied by millions of the toughest warriors of any species in the known galaxy. That is a resource we could use, don't you think?"

Gur didn't seem entirely convinced, but he didn't reply. The rider of the Ejdar pointed for them to reduce altitude and follow him. They were led through a vast rocky canyon, beneath an overpass, and into a corridor that had been cut through a dense forest of trees. It looked so barbed and sharp that they would tear flesh from the bone with any contact with your skin.

"They choose to live here?"

Jafar was amazed to hear Gur speak so many words, but he could understand why. Many of the Krys led a harsh existence on worlds that were far from easy to live on, but they seemed nothing compared to the environment they had now entered. An Ejdar appeared through an opening in the woods as though intending to lash out at their craft, but the Ejdar rider ahead drew out a spear and launched it at the creature as if it were a typical sight. The spear hit the Ejdar in the chest and penetrated half a metre. The Ejdar staggered back a little until a tree stopped it.

Their craft passed the beast, but Gur looked through the aft porthole. It gripped the spear in its jaws and pulled it from its body, continuing on as if nothing had occurred.

"What do you think it takes to make one of those your own?"

"Guess you just have to demonstrate who's in charge and show no fear," replied Jafar, as he looked at the formidable beast flying ahead of them. "You can see the appeal, can't you?" he whispered, "Power, freedom. They have far more than you might first realise."

"You talk like this is some sort of paradise."

"To some, Boz, I believe it is."

The path opened out into a vast circular area. It was surrounded by a ten metre high stonewall that had clearly been built with hard graft. It looked more like an arena than anything else. The rider signalled for them to follow him down, and Boz obliged. They were soon on the ground, and the door opened for them to acquire their first smell of Erzurum air. Jafar knew what was coming, but he was still not prepared for its acrid nature. There was an acidic taste that burnt the nostrils and scorched the eyes.

Boz and Gur went to activate their helmets contained within their suits, as Jafar's was.

"No," he stated firmly, "They already think we are soft and weak. Do not give them any further reason to believe so."

He stepped out onto the ramp and down to the large arena. The ground was hard, almost like rock. He couldn't believe anything could actually grow or live there, and yet that explained the harshness of everything they had seen. He knew every living thing in that planet had evolved through such adversity that only the toughest would make it.

The Ejdars landed just fifteen metres away, and the Barbarlar rider leapt off with ease. His armour covered most of his body, with overlapping blades seemingly made of hard skin or bone. A pistol hung at his waist, and yet it was dusty and likely saw little use. He carried a small axe and a cudgel on his back, and they could see a glaive like weapon slung under the saddle on the Ejdar. None of his close quarter weapons appeared to be powered.

Jafar could see his two bodyguards didn't understand why the Barbarlars chose to live such a primitive existence, when they had access to technology far beyond what they appeared to utilise.

"You wish an audience with the Barbs?" asked the rider.

"I do," replied Jafar.

"The Grand Siparis Coskun will see you, but be wary you do not issue insult, for he is not forgiving."

"Yes, I am aware."

Although he was thinking what Taylor would have said in his usual dismissive and sarcastic tone. He almost went as far as saying it, but he kept it within his own mind.

No shit!

The rider drew out a horn from his side and blew into it. The deep warble echoed around the vast open topped arena until it fell silent once more. Boz and Gur looked suspicious and turned constantly, expecting to find a threat or ambush of some kind.

"Be calm," said Jafar, "There are things of this world that you never thought possible, things long forgotten to the Krys people. They may look like us, but we have long since parted their ways. Stay calm, and do nothing."

The Barb rider looked at Jafar with suspicion, holding onto his every word, as if not recognising the language and trying to make some sense of it. He seemed to hold a position of power, but nothing near Jafar's level, and yet he looked down on the Lord as if he meant nothing at all. Jafar could tell the situation was already highly volatile and so kept his calm.

They could now hear the flutter of heavy wings from dozens of Ejdars. The trees around the outskirts were fluttering as they flew close to the canopy and soared into view. Twenty of the beasts came in to land, some with individual riders, others with up to five Barbarlars on their backs. More of the Barbs came rushing in through small entrances around the perimeter. Some carried rifles, but most just held spears and bladed weapons.

The Ejdars landed in a fifty-metre crescent around their position.

Whoever the savage creatures are, they are well trained and disciplined.

Though just as he thought it, one of them reached

around to try and take a bite out of the rider that had just leapt off. The Barbarlar warrior casually punched it on the top of the head. It slumped slightly, accepting his will and drooping its head in submission. Jafar wasn't sure whether to respect or pity them.

A few moments passed as the Ejdar riders stood silently watching them like hawks. The other two looked uneasy, but Jafar knew what was coming, as he had been here with Erdogan once before. He had witnessed how intimidating the Barbarlar Lords could be, and he would not make the same mistakes his predecessor did. The roar of a large creature filled the air from over the treetops. It was as loud as it was coarse and almost burst their eardrums. Seconds later, the huge beast swept into view and swooped in, landing smoothly in the middle of the circle a few metres from them and their shuttle.

The Ejdar was twice the size of all others. This was a powerful leader, and the Barbarlar they needed to talk to. Despite the heavy creature's smooth landing, it sent vibrations through the ground as it came to a standstill. Its body and wings were painted in bright blue stripes, the only done in this manner. The skulls of a dozen Krys hung from a chain running around its neck. The rider wore a cloak made of some garish multi coloured animal hide and a cloak of thorny branches and teeth. Jafar began to wonder if this could ever have been a good idea, but both Taylor and Irala wanted it, and that was enough.

Jafar felt the weight of the creature's breath as it snorted before him. It stank like nothing he had smelt in a few hundred years. The rider seemed to let the beast weigh him up for a moment; then jumped down and stepped up before him. He was larger than the average Barbarlar, and that meant he stood over Jafar, much like he always towered over Taylor. He was starting to get a feel for how that might have felt all those years ago.

He wore the torso armour of a Krys Lord, much like Erdogan had, no doubt pillaged from one that he had killed. The rest of his armour was made from animal skin and bonded layers of animal skin and bone. Long locks of hair flowed from his brow and would have been pure white, were it not for the dirt and dust particles. He looked like some bizarre circus creation to Jafar, but also a very strong and unforgiving one.

"I am Siparis Coskun, Lord of all Barbarlars," he stated proudly.

Jafar almost laughed, for he sounded even more anachronistic and absurd than he had expected, but he knew he must remain calm.

"Lord Jafar, of the Krys unified worlds."

Coskun looked at him seriously for just a moment. He then turned away and walked a few places, erupting into a deep laugh.

"What do you want?"

"I am here to make you an offer that will assist all our

worlds," Jafar said loudly and firmly.

"No offworlder ever travels here without wanting something. You did not come here for our benefit. What is it that you want of us?" he roared.

Jafar sighed, for he could see Coskun was far smarter than he had hoped.

"An enemy threatens us all; all our worlds, Krys, Human, Aranui, and Cholan. They will be on your doorstep soon. I propose an alliance that is beneficial to us all."

"What happens off world is of no concern of ours."

"But it will be your concern, and you will not be strong enough alone."

Coskun spun around in anger.

"Not strong enough!" he roared even louder.

Laughter rang out from those surrounding them. Jafar could not help but feel pity. They were all strong and brave people, but they had no understanding of what they would be facing before long.

"They are too strong for all of us. A dozen worlds of the best Krys fighters you have ever known would not be enough."

"And you want our help, but why? Why would we give it?"

Jafar knew he had to take a different road to convince them.

"Because you enjoy war more than peace, you hone your skills in combat, and because you never walk away from a challenge. I am offering you the greatest challenge you have ever known."

Coskun laughed once more, but Jafar didn't understand why until he finally responded. The rest of them carried on laughing until their leader lifted his hand to call for silence.

"If this enemy is so powerful, such a worthy challenge, and that they will find us soon enough, why would we bother leaving our world? We can stay home and await the inevitable."

Jafar shook his head, realising what a corner he had backed himself into.

"So, Lord Jafar, the real reason you are here is in plain sight."

Oh, no!

"Your people are weak. Your Alliance is weak. You turn to us because you are desperate, and do you know what I say to you?"

Jafar shook his head, but he could already see what was coming. Coskun strolled back and forth before his people. He was playing to the crowd, and Jafar knew it was at his expense.

"You have led the Krys people into weakness. But I would not have them weak. As a Lord of the Krys, I invoke my birth privilege and challenge you for the leadership of our people!"

Jafar had never thought the man so intelligent, or power

hungry. He fully expected to be ambushed or killed, but not to have to face an enemy as intelligent as he was strong. He never expected for a moment that any Barbarlar could have his eye on the leadership of the Krys people.

"For thousands of years you have chosen to remain isolated, and with no interest in the lives of any Krys that were not your own, why now?"

Coskun ignored the question, strode back to his mount, and drew out a large Bardiche from his saddle. The weapon was almost three metres long. The shaft ran most of the length, and the agile looking axe blade almost a metre long and stretching to a wicked point.

"Surrender your title to me, or fight for it!" he stated.

He turned, looked to his people, and thrust his Bardiche into the air.

"I claim the title of Overlord over all the Krys people!"

They roared with excitement, and Jafar knew he had no choice now. He turned back to Boz and Gur who looked ready and willing to raise their rifles. Jafar opened his mouth to tell them no, but it was too late. They both raised the muzzles of their weapons to take aim at the enemy leader. Seemingly out of nowhere a spear struck Boz. It pierced his armour at the shoulder and drove deep into his body. He cried out in agony as the rifle fell from his hands. Gur turned as he heard his friend cry in pain, and in that brief moment, the Ejdar rider who had led them there struck him in the back with a large two-handed cudgel.

The impact was strong enough to launch him off his feet and caused him to land face first on the hard rock. He turned around just in time to see the cudgel smash down on his head. He went limp. Jafar couldn't tell if he was dead or not, but it didn't seem to matter anymore.

"Die a warrior or a coward, it is your choice," Coskun declared.

Jafar nodded in acceptance and drew out the glaive from his back. He activated the mechanism, and it extended out to two metres in length. A large disk shape hand shield expanded out from the shaft. He did not power up the weapon, not wanting to be seen to be cheating with the use of advanced technology. Coskun moved back and beckoned for Jafar to follow him out into the middle of the arena, away from the bodies and Ejdars.

Coskun stretched out his arms and held the massive Bardiche as if it weighed nothing at all. The audience around them shouted with excitement.

At least this is a good way to die, Jafar thought.

But he wasn't willing to go down easily. He stopped, took up a fighting stance, and waited for Coskun. He was still pandering to the crowd. Finally, he turned and rushed towards Jafar. He swung a heavy two-handed horizontal cut. Jafar backed off, but Coskun kept coming and swung the blade around his head, smashing it down with an earth shattering vertical cut. Jafar narrowly avoided it with another step back. The blade struck the ground so hard it would have cut him in two had it found its target.

"You are fast," stated Coskun, sounding surprised, "Good, I would be disappointed for this to end with so little effort."

Jafar felt the pain of his flank wound biting into his side. His pain receptors were on fire, and yet he hid it perfectly. He had always been a fast fighter, and he had lost little over time, despite his age. Coskun came at him again with a heavy horizontal cut. He carried the blade around in a full arch and delivered three identical cuts as Jafar backed off. On the third, Jafar ducked under and sliced into his opponent's thigh as he passed him.

Coskun stumbled slightly before regaining his footing. He made no cry in pain. He turned and growled in anger before looking down at the wound. He seemed more surprised than hurt. He took up his weapon and rushed forward, lunging with the mighty blade. Jafar parried the blade to one side, but his opponent swung it back on the opposing line. He parried just in time, and the blade smashed into the hand guard and crushed it almost flat against the shaft of the glaive.

Their weapons were locked against one another now. Coskun pushed forward and shoved Jafar back. He was lifted off his feet and staggered a few paces back before regaining his balance. Coskun was far stronger, but he could not match Jafar's speed. But as Jafar came to a standstill, he winced in pain as the wound at his flank opened from the strain of the fight.

Coskun could see the blood seeping through Jafar's armour now and smiled, realising how vulnerable Jafar was. There was no hiding it anymore. He went forward and cut down to bind with Jafar, who slid his blade past and slashed across Coskun's face. The slice opened a deep cut from the cheek to the side of his mouth, but he ran the Bardiche down Jafar's weapon until the blade cut in and locked against the glaive. He placed his left hand on the haft, and then pulled with both until the glaive was prised from Jafar's hands.

The Barbarlar Lord, now with both weapons, stood triumphantly and confidently before him. But Jafar did not accept defeat. He knew he had a short opening, for carrying both large weapons was cumbersome and unwieldy. He ran forwards and jumped to drive a knee into Coskun. It impacted hard enough to drive him back a step, and he had no choice but to drop both weapons in an attempt to defend himself.

Jafar followed it with an elbow to Coskun's face. The impact snapped his head to one side, but he came back quickly with a hammer blow heading for Jafar's neck. He parried it just in time but was driven down to one knee by the power of the strike. Coskun seized his opportunity and kicked heavily into Jafar's seeping wound. He could not help but let out a squirm in agony as the pain shot through his body. But he fought through it and kicked to the inside of Coskun's thigh, and then drove an uppercut into his jaw. It knocked him back a few paces.

As he got up, he saw the worry in Coskun's face. This fight had not gone half as easy as he had expected it to. Jafar had honed his fighting prowess over hundreds of years and countless battles, and Coskun was just starting to realise it. He looked a little desperate and peered around at the audience. They were watching in amazement that he was struggling so badly.

"What's the matter? Can't beat an old man?" Jafar asked sarcastically.

He knew it was just the kind of antagonistic statement that Taylor would make. It was the benchmark to work from. He had never known a more successful being than Taylor, and truly believed he was one to be followed. Coskun was looking down at a part of his armour on his right forearm as if contemplating something. He looked worried now. His body language was different. His shoulders were slightly slumped, and his stance not so aggressive.

He reached to his forearm with his left hand and drew something out. It was a tiny push dagger that he clenched tight into his grip. It was so small he could barely see it now, and there was no chance the rest of the Barbarlars would be able to. He came forward at Jafar once again and jabbed with his left. Jafar dodged the first two and ducked under the third. He punched into the neck of Coskun, but as he staggered back, he swung clumsily with his left, and the tip of the punch dagger sliced ever so slightly into Jafar's chin.

Jafar stopped for a moment and felt the light trickle of blood down his neck. He could smell something bizarre, a repulsive and toxic scent that appeared to be mixing with the blood of his wound. Coskun had a wicked smirk on his face.

"Ejdar bile. They use it to weaken their prey. How do you feel now, Lord Jafar?"

He felt his mind slowing down and his vision blurring slightly, as if he was highly intoxicated. Coskun rushed towards him. He managed to duck under one strike, but once again took a kick into the wound in his flank. He keeled over and Coskun's iron like fist connected with the side of his head. He landed hard on the ground and turned over to see a foot about to flatten his face. He rolled out of the way and stood up, staggering slightly, not able to maintain his balance. Coskun circled him now, as if cautiously waiting the right moment to take down an injured beast that was still a threat. Jafar simply stood up straight and began to laugh with a deep and echoing tone that was unsettling to all.

"The mighty Lord of the Barbarlars couldn't beat me in a fair fight," he added, as he continued to laugh.

He knew it would mean little to those who watched.

They had no reason to believe his words, but it was how damaging it was to Coskun's ego that made him laugh. In a fit of anger, the Barb Lord rushed forwards and swung a heavy punch to Jafar's face. He was suffering the effects of the toxin too badly to move in time, and his head jerked to the side from the impact, but he was still defiant. He immediately swung back with all he had and delivered a similar strike to Coskun, but his right leg gave out. He didn't feel it immediately as the toxin had dulled his senses.

Down on one knee and defeated, he looked up at the Barbarlar with disdain and defiance in his eyes.

"You are a fraud."

He punched with all his force into Jafar's face, and he went down. He lay on his side barely conscious, watching Coskun stride over and retrieve his Bardiche from the ground. He returned to finish him off.

"No!" cried a voice.

The weapon was held above the Lord's head ready to execute Jafar in one strike. But the rider of the Ejdar who first greeted them rushed into view.

"Honour has been satisfied. You know our laws as well as any."

Coskun looked furious and contemplated ignoring the statement, but finally threw his weapon aside. Jafar knew that however savage the Barbarlars might be, they supported their leaders through a strict code, and that had saved his life this day.

"Fine, let him rot like the disgraced fool he is. To the pits with him."

CHAPTER FIVE

Sarik paced restlessly from one side of the bridge to the other. He stopped and looked at the time. Twenty-five hours had passed. Everyone there knew what standing order Jafar had given before leaving, but nobody wanted to raise the question of whether they should fulfil it, knowing that to do so meant abandoning their leader. It seemed like Sarik would be willing to wait forever for Jafar. The comms officer finally broke the silence.

"What are your orders, Sir?" he asked.

Sarik kept thinking and said nothing.

"Sir, about Lord Jafar's order?"

Still he said nothing.

"Sir, we cannot remain here forever."

Sarik opened his mouth to speak, but before he could say a word, a light flashed and a buzzer rang to denote they were being hailed.

"Put them through!" he yelled, excited and concerned all at the same time.

The Barbarlar who had first greeted them was displayed before him once more.

"Where is Lord Jafar?" Sarik asked impatiently.

"Lord Coskun is your leader now, and you and the rest of the Krys people are required to swear allegiance to him immediately."

Sarik looked furious. His grip tightened around the sidearm he carried as he felt the need for violence.

"I swear allegiance to no one but Lord Jafar!" he spat back.

The Barbarlar stayed calm and did nothing to provoke a violent response.

"Jafar has been beaten in a fair and legal challenge, an ancient right that my Lord invoked. The law of our people requires that you swear allegiance to him."

Sarik shook his head in disbelief.

"Never," he snarled, "Never will I accept your master as my own, and I will die before I see the day that a single other Krys world does."

"They you would defy the laws of your people?"

"I would defy the wretched barbarian scum that is your master. Return Lord Jafar to me, or incur my wrath."

The Barbarlar laughed and ended the transmission. Sarik looked to his crew for information.

"They are heading back to Erzurum."

Sarik sighed.

"What do we do?" the pilot asked.

"There is nothing we can do right now. We do not have the strength to attack, and they know it. Set a course for Ares 4. I don't know how, but we are going to get Jafar back."

"How do you even know he is alive?"

"Because those are our laws, cast down from every generation of Krys, and even those savages believe them."

He stared at the viewscreen showing the planet and thought what state Jafar might be in.

"I will come back," he whispered.

The engines fired up, and the ship banked to come about. Sarik could not help but feel hopeless, but he knew just where to go for help. Jafar had always told him to trust in Taylor, so that was precisely what he would do.

* * *

Irala stood on the bridge of the Ares 4 station, in temporary command of both the station and what remained of the fleet. Human and Krys crew worked all around him trying to restore the hardware and patch up all they could. He was under no illusion that they had taken a beating. The doors to the bridge opened, and to everyone's surprise, it was the President of the Alliance. One of the bridge crew called everyone to attention, but Irala never cared for such formalities.

"I am glad to see you are recovering well," he said to Isaacs.

"Thank you, Chancellor. I needed to get on my own two feet and see it all for myself," he replied, strolling forward and staring in shock at the devastation of the fleet visible from the vast windows. Last time he had been there the blast doors were shut and he could see little, but now the full extent of it was clear.

"You look at figures on paper, losses, wounded, but none of it means much until you see it for yourself."

"The Cholans are a desperate people, driven to desperate measures."

"We cannot afford any more of this division in the Alliance. We are ripping each other apart."

"Yes, they did the wrong thing for the right reasons, as Mitch Taylor would say."

"What?" Isaacs asked.

He ignored the comment. It meant little to him, and Irala cared little to explain it.

"We have a gateway opening," said Lieutenant Bravos.

They both looked to the image of the gateway and could see that it was not active.

"Where?" Isaacs asked in a panic.

Lights flashed, and a gateway opened less than a kilometre in front of them. Everyone was silent and waited for some sign of what was coming through. A dozen Cholan warships finally surged through into view, and the crew went rigid with terror.

"It's over," whispered Isaacs.

But seconds later they saw three Human vessels pass through, surrounded by many more Cholan ships.

"What is that?"

"I believe that is Taylor," replied Irala.

"What? How?"

"We're being hailed by the Guam, Sir," stated Bravos.

"Put them through!" Isaacs snapped.

A projection lit up before them, and to their amazement and joy, it was indeed Taylor.

"How is this possible?"

"I went to do a job, and I got it done. That's how it is possible. Do you have faith now?" Taylor asked.

His tone was a little angry and disrespectful of the President, and yet Isaacs was too shocked and happy to notice.

"What are the intentions of the Cholan Empire now?" Irala added more seriously.

"Yes, yes, what are they going to do now?"

"Whatever we tell them, Mr President," replied Taylor.

Isaacs shook his head in disbelief.

"You've only just joined this new life, and you have already subdued and conquered an entire race!"

Taylor smiled in response to Irala, though he knew that

was not the tone it was meant in.

"If this is what you are capable of today, what will you do tomorrow?"

He wasn't sure if Irala was impressed or shocked over what he had done.

"I'm coming over," he replied and ended the transmission.

"How does he do it?"

Irala looked concerned, something Isaacs had never seen from him before.

"What is it?" he asked.

"You will soon have to make a decision."

The President looked on intensely and waited for him to continue; the pause was killing him.

"You must decide whether you are willing to hand over power to the Colonel."

"Hand over power? What on Earth are you talking about?"

"Do you not see? Mitch Taylor has not won this battle for you. He has won it for the Alliance."

"I don't see what you are getting at. I am in charge of the Alliance."

Irala shook his head.

"The Colonel has always done what he considers best, whether those above him like it or not. And now he has the entire Cholan Empire loyal to him."

"Loyal to the Alliance," Isaacs replied firmly.

Irala didn't bother responding, for he knew the President would not heed his advice.

Taylor and his team of Immortals sat along one side of the shuttle, with as many Cholans opposite them. At their centre was the new Emperor, Tuin. He had donned the purple sash of the Emperor, but in all other regards was dressed and equipped as when he and Taylor first met and exchanged blows.

"You will still not wear the crown?" Taylor asked.

Tuin shook his head.

"Why?" asked Babacan.

"Because I want to be the kind of Emperor I always wanted to follow."

Taylor appreciated the sentiment and that he and Tuin were not a world apart. Although he did not envy the responsibility the Cholan had now taken on as a result of his actions.

"You came to my world to ensure the Cholan people support the Alliance against the Morohta, but do I have your word you will see this through, for all our sakes?"

Taylor nodded and offered out his hand. Tuin still looked a little suspicious, and he had every right to be. Despite Taylor's hatred of what so many Cholans had done to him and those around him, he remembered the day he accepted Jafar amongst them, and it had paid off in dividends until this very day.

The ship passed into the docking bay of the Ares space

station. Hundreds of crewmembers were lined up to great them in a lavish ceremony. Many more were still working to repair the station and craft beyond. Taylor was already shaking his head.

"Still don't get it do they?" he muttered.

"Get what?" Alita asked.

"That we don't have time for all this. A hundred personnel standing around doing nothing is the sort of waste of resources we cannot afford."

She didn't know how to respond. The shuttle came to a landing, and the ramp lowered. A red carpet led to where the President awaited them. A roar of applause rang out as he came into view, but he found it hard to be appreciative. He leapt down with his Immortals and strode towards the President. Irala was standing beside him.

"You've done a fine job, Colonel. You have pulled off the impossible!" Isaacs yelled with a huge grin on his face.

"Sir, can we please give up all the kissing ass and get down to business?"

The President looked as surprised as he was offended. He leaned in close to Taylor to whisper in his ear as the applause continued.

"Look at them. They need this once in a while. A victory. They have led miserable lives since all this began. Let them enjoy your success."

For once he stood back and was silenced. Isaacs had a point, and he felt a little sheepish for being so dismissive of the welcome party. He looked around at all their faces to see they genuinely were exuberant. He nodded to accept the applause and slowly smiled in response.

"Now can we get back to business?" he finally asked with a smile.

The President raised his hand to call for silence and then pointed for Taylor to speak to them.

"May I present to you, the new leader of the Cholan Empire, Emperor Tuin!"

The Cholan appeared at the door of the craft to everyone's surprise, along with a dozen of his personal staff and soldiers. Isaacs was shocked to the core.

"What happened to Kuyok?" he whispered to Taylor.

"He isn't a problem anymore."

Isaacs still look confused until Jones leaned in close to whisper back.

"What the Colonel is trying to say politely is that he put a bullet between his eyes."

Isaacs' eyes widened, and he went pale.

"Colonel, you can't just kill an Emperor!"

"This is war. The winner makes the rules."

Jones still shook his head that Taylor had even contemplated regicide, let alone gone through with it and with no regrets at all. Taylor pointed back to Tuin as if for Isaacs to acknowledge him, and finally he did so. He coughed to clear his throat and recover from the shocking news.

"Emperor, welcome to Ares 4. Please come aboard."

They exchanged pleasantries for just a few seconds when Isaacs beckoned for them to follow him.

"Please, we have much to discuss."

Taylor gestured for Jones, Alita, and Babacan to join him.

"Uhhh, this is a briefing for high-ranking government officials and commanding officers only," stated Isaacs.

"Where I go, they go," Taylor replied forcefully.

Isaacs submitted quickly. Taylor could see he was still not a man to be fully trusted, and he never wanted to be anywhere without someone protecting his back. They were led through to a large conference room. It was in impeccable condition, as if untouched by the battle. Hardly surprising; they had passed through many corridors into the heart of the station to reach the highly protected and secure facility. A dozen guards stood watch over the entrance, half Human, half Krys.

Upon stepping inside they found just a handful of officers there. Isaacs and Irala were the only VIPs Taylor recognised.

"Please, take a seat," Isaacs said to Tuin.

The President seemed a little intimidated by the Cholan. That was hardly surprising, for despite his size he looked as combat hardened as Taylor. They each took their seats while Taylor's comrades stood at his back as guards, just as each of the political representatives and high-ranking officials had.

"Gentlemen, I have assembled you here in part to renew the treaty of the Alliance. Also to assure everyone that it will return to the founding principles in which it was created, and to establish a way forward."

Taylor looked around the room at the many empty seats. A high number of important representatives were killed in the last battle, and that put everyone on edge, but he was keen to hear what the President had in mind.

"First and foremost, we have come to this place and this position because of the aggression of the Morohta people. They will not be bargained with, and I accept that now, as I believe we all do. All efforts must now move to the defences of the Alliance so that we may be ready for the coming of the Morohta fleets."

Taylor was glad to hear the President finally committing to what they needed and listened intently as he continued.

"With that purpose in mind, we must no longer risk any person or resource at our disposal until the day comes that we must fight the Morohta. There will be no more conflict within the Alliance. Colonel Taylor has already shown what will happen to those who break under the will of the enemy, and do not stand beside us when we need them most."

Taylor smiled at the prospect of him being the sword dangling over those heads that considered dissent. A light began flashing on a console beside the President. He could not ignore it, for it was clearly something of great importance. He accepted the message. It was Lieutenant Bravos.

"Mr President, the Yavuz has returned. Commander Sarik has requested to speak to you personally."

Taylor's smile turned to serious concern. He could not understand how it would be Sarik making contact unless something had gone badly wrong.

"Put the Commander through."

Taylor was surprised the President was having the communication in full view of them all, but pleasantly surprised. Sarik appeared projected before them, and even though he was side on to the Colonel, he saw the dire concern in his face.

"Where is Lord Jafar?" Isaacs asked.

Sarik replied dryly and with bitterness.

"My Lord has been deposed by the leader of the Barbarlars, just as he feared, and yet you sent him anyway."

"It was the right move, and you know it," replied Taylor.

Sarik did not respond.

"Are the Barbarlars going to join our cause?"

Sarik shook his head. "They want no further communication with the Alliance, and their leader has assumed Lord Jafar's position as the leader of our people. Whether they will accept him, I do not know."

"Well, what does this mean?"

"It means the Krys people are divided, as we may see

no support at all," snapped Taylor.

Isaacs gasped in shock soon turned to Taylor with a blameful look in his eye.

"This is on you. You sent Jafar to that system. For all your efforts to get the Cholans back, and you have just lost a far stronger ally!"

Taylor could not believe his tone. He could feel his blood boiling and wanted nothing more than to wrap his fingers around the President's throat. Yet he knew he could not. He kicked back his chair and stood up, turning to leave the room.

"Where are you going?" Isaacs demanded.

Taylor stopped, considering his words carefully before looking back in disgust.

"I am going to sort this mess out."

"You will do no such thing! I order you to stand down, and sit back down at this table!" Isaacs leapt out of his chair.

Sarik intervened and broke the few seconds of suspenseful silence.

"I will support you in whatever course of action you take, if it involves getting Jafar back and returning him to his rightful position."

Isaacs could not believe what he was hearing, but before he could respond, the newly appointed Cholan stood up to have his say. Isaacs waited to hear him out, as they all did.

"Colonel Taylor, you have my support and my fleet. This Alliance has been weakened too much already, and I trust that you will do everything necessary to keep it strong."

Taylor nodded in gratitude and looked back to Isaacs. The President turned to Irala for support, but the ambassador did nothing. Irala's warning was making some sense to him now. He looked around and realised he had no power in the room anymore. He was completely at the will of a single colonel. He shook his head in disbelief and slumped down into his chair.

"Clearly I can do nothing to stop you. Just please do what is best for the Alliance, and not what is best to save one friend."

"In this instance, they are one and the same," replied Taylor.

The President shrugged, accepting the scenario. Taylor turned to Tuin.

"If we were to mount an all-out offensive on the Barbarlar world, how long would you need to get your fleet combat ready?"

"Even what we have left will need several weeks of refits before they are back to fully serviceable order."

"We are all in much the same position. That last battle cost us dearly," replied Isaacs.

"I don't intend to fight another. I just want enough of a show of force."

"That will mean nothing to the Barbarlars," replied Sarik, "They will want that fight. They live for it."

"I said I am not looking for a war. I just want them to take us seriously. How quickly can you get me a fleet of thirty ships that at least look fully serviceable? The kind of fleet that looks like it is meant for invasion."

"Crews are already working around the clock," replied Isaacs, "We could spare maybe ten if you give us seventy-two hours to get them in a fit state."

Taylor looked to Sarik and Tuin.

"Can you match that?"

Both of them nodded in agreement.

"Then you each have seventy-two hours, and not a minute longer."

He couldn't believe what he had just done. It was sinking in now that he had just put out his orders to the whole Alliance, a situation that made him the de facto leader of all the aligned worlds. It sent a shiver down his spine to be put in a position of such responsibility, but he could see it was what they needed.

"What else do you need?" Irala asked.

"I need more men and women under my command, my regiment. I have just a handful, and no matter how elite they are, I need the best. The marines from the Guam proved themselves in combat. See their ranks are replenished with experienced troops and brought up to our standard of hardware, think you can do that, Mr President?"

The President turned to a Naval officer standing at his side. She had kept out of the whole argument. The woman had been promoted far above her station in the wake of the battle and was still stunned by the whole thing.

"Commander?"

"Ye....yes, Colonel, I am sure we can do that."

"Good, then make sure that you do."

He turned to leave when the President stood up abruptly.

"Where are you going?"

Taylor turned back.

"Me and my people have fought two battles without rest. The stims will only keep them on their feet for so long. We will be needed again once this operation gets underway. Until then, this is on the rest of you."

He turned and left with his small posse at his side. As they got out of the door, Alita began to laugh.

"You just put a beat down on the President of the Alliance, and you didn't even have to throw a punch," she joked.

"Yes, I never thought negotiation was something you had in you," added Jones.

Taylor shrugged and smiled. "Somebody gonna make a joke about an old dog and new tricks now?"

They laughed it off as they split off to find their quarters until it was just Taylor and Alita left.

"Been waiting for this moment for a long time," she

said.

As they reached Taylor's quarters and the doors opened, she pushed him inside. They each stripped off their armoured suits, and the second they hit the floor, she took a running jump onto Taylor with her legs wrapped around his waist. He gasped a little as his sore legs ached, but the pain was soon replaced with pleasure as she kissed him, and he sat back down on the bed with her straddling him.

* * *

Three days R&R passed quickly. Taylor had barely left his room for anything but to find food and drink when the time finally came. He was amazed they were not called to some new disaster in that time, but in every moment he thought about his friend, wondering if he were still alive. There was just one hour left to the deadline he had set when he pulled on his armour and went onto the docking bay to rendezvous with his people. Alita was close by his side, and he looked across to her. Her armour was as worn and scratched as his now. She looked every bit the combat veteran that she had become.

"Not quite the job you expected when you trained to be a pilot, is it?"

She shook her head and smiled.

"No, but there's no place I'd rather be."

"On the frontline with a rifle in hand?"

She shook her head.

"No, by your side."

Taylor couldn't answer, but it brought a smile to his face as they stepped into the hangar bay. The rest of the Immortals were sitting around casually, waiting for him. Jones shouted to call them to attention, but he waved the command off and let them be.

"You all know who Lord Jafar is today. But he is far more than his title and his position. Along with his brothers-in-arms, he was the first Krys to come over to us. He joined the Immortals and became one our very best. None of you lived in those days, but I can tell you, he is as much a part of the Immortals as I am, and now you are, too. He is a brother, and we will never leave a brother to such a fate. Load up, and let's go bring him home."

The weariness in their faces had gone now after the few days' rest. A new enthusiasm had grown inside them, and they were starting to believe they could and were making a difference. Antos began to clap and was soon followed by the others. Many of the ship's crew around them were stunned and just watched. Taylor went forward to the shuttle that awaited them, and they followed suit. Time passed quickly as Taylor fell into a daydream as he considered all the pressures upon him. The next thing he knew they were making their landing aboard the Guam, and he was glad to see there was no ceremony waiting for them, only marines assembling for combat.

He stepped aboard and gestured for his people to stay put. He carried on to the bridge with Jones, where he found Captain Song making last minute checks with her flight crew.

"Still working here, Captain?"

"I have been assigned to the Guam on a permanent basis. This ship is now my home," she replied firmly.

"And I am glad to hear it. You did a damn fine job at Yaxha."

"But the vessel is still bearing the scars."

Taylor looked around the bridge. Many parts had been hastily repaired, and loose cabling still trailed across the deck where anything and everything had been done to keep her in service.

"She's a tough old girl. I wouldn't want to be anywhere else."

"If I may ask, why are we not jumping directly to the Barbarlar world with the use of the Aranui jump technology, as we have before?"

"We're taking a lot of ships with us, and Ares needs as much protection as we can afford to leave behind. The Aranui vessels are still the most powerful in the fleet, besides the Nakbe, which will also stay behind. Also, I want the Barbarlars to know we are coming."

"You do not want the element of surprise?" she asked, after the manner in which they had conducted their last mission.

Taylor shook his head.

"If I wanted a battle or a war, yes, but I do not. We cannot afford it."

"Why do we not do what we did before, and strike at the heart, like you did the Cholans?"

Taylor took a deep breath. He hadn't even considered it, but he knew deep down the reason.

"Because the Cholans are a people that could be easily forced to submit. The Krys are not, and from what I hear of these Barbarlars, it is far worse. They will drag us into a war that will not end anytime soon. If we kill their leader in any way other than through a manner they respect and can accept, the whole lot will come down on us."

"You know this?"

Taylor shrugged. "As much as any of us can know anything."

"That's reassuring," Jones muttered.

Taylor heard and looked around. The Lieutenant was smiling and had merely meant it in jest.

"Then how will you manage it?" Song asked, "If these aren't the sort of people to be reasoned with or threatened, what will you do?"

"I've got an idea."

Jones was already shaking his head, and Song looked to him for answers.

"I can't even imagine, but you're not going to like it."

"Colonel, we have already lost Lord Jafar to this world. Please do not sacrifice yourself in the same manner."

"Trust me, I don't intend to."

"I am not even sure what the chain of command is anymore," stated Song.

Taylor agreed, for lines were blurred at best.

"Commander Sarik will lead this fleet. He is the highest ranking officer and deserves the chance to lead his people back there to get Jafar back, but ground operations will be by my authority."

She nodded in agreement, but then frowned as she thought it through further.

"What of the Cholan emperor?"

"Tuin is here to support and oversee operations. He has no military title or position."

Taylor rested back against a console near the Captain's chair and marvelled at the fleet they had assembled. He knew that in reality the whole lot of them were loyal to him, and he was all that held them altogether. Jones was doing the same.

"Amazing, isn't it? I wake up and am told of this peaceful Utopia where there are no wars and everyone gets along, and yet the minute something rocks the boat, everyone is at each other's throats. Things haven't changed as much as most people think."

Jones nodded.

"Every generation wants to think those who lived

before them were more primitive, more violent, less advanced, and less sophisticated in their society."

Taylor smiled.

"You sound just like Charlie."

Jones appreciated that, but it still meant little to him.

"I still cannot get my head around the fact you knew an ancestor of mine that not a single relative alive in my lifetime has ever met. It is not natural."

"No, but there are many unnatural things in this life, and clearly they aren't all bad. You know the first time I saw a Krys warrior and fought them with firearms; you would consider it a joke today. We could barely penetrate their armour. They were terrifying and immortal creatures. It seemed as if they would sweep across the world and end humanity for good. Look where we are now. We consider one another equals, and we are risking everything to save one of them."

"I never understood why the Krys fought us the way they did."

"Because you never met those who led them. The royal bloodline that ruled over them with an iron fist was a cruel and sadistic hand. Pray you never see the day you have to come face-to-face with some monster like Erdogan."

"I wish I could say I haven't."

And then it struck him.

Ganbaatar.

In all the hectic battles with the Cholans, he had let

himself forget the Morohta Prince.

"Next time we will be ready," said Taylor.

"We have the signal from Commander Sarik. The fleet is prepared to move out," said Nichols.

Song glanced to Taylor for confirmation, and he simply nodded to give the go ahead. They could see the jump gate opening.

"Take us out," ordered Song.

CHAPTER SIX

Jafar looked up to the small hole in the ceiling, the only source of daylight. The toxins had long since worn off, but he had lost track of how many days he had been there as a result of their effects. He was sitting against a damp wall and had been stripped of his armour. He wore just the skin-tight compression suit that still had the gaping hole and bandage over his flank. He peeled it back. The wound was healing quickly, and he no longer winced in pain as he moved.

He heard something slide across the floor. A wooden tray bumped across the ground and stopped a metre away from him. It was the same god-awful food he had been living on since he arrived. Some kind of primitive bread denser than an overcooked steak, and a slime that barely seemed edible at all. Years of living a life of luxury had not let him forget the bad times, and he would weather them once again. He picked up the plate and looked up at the Barbarlar guard who had thrown it at him. He stood behind prison bars woven together from a local vine that seemed as strong as tempered steel. Every part of life was tough on this planet, and he could see what it had done to those that inhabited the savage land.

The guard looked at him with disgust, as if insulted by his lavish and decadent ways. But Jafar would have none of it. He picked up the bread and chewed down on it as if it were any other meal, refusing to be seen as weak amongst anyone, let alone the savages now imprisoning him. He got halfway through the food, and the guard had not left; yet he always had within seconds before. He knew something was different this time. He could hear footsteps approaching and stopped eating so that he may listen and watch intently.

Two other guards strode into view on the other side of the bars. They hauled Boz and Gur alongside them, with their hands bound in a thick twine. Both looked battered and bloody, and with barely enough energy to walk. They were dragging their feet and completely unable to resist. Jafar brought his legs back and began to get up when the guard shouted at him.

"Stay!"

The command disgusted him. He was being treated like an enslaved animal, but there was nothing he could do to change their situation. All he could do was wait and hope someone would come for him. Part of him wished he had not sent Sarik away, but had he not, it would only have condemned him and so many more to the same fate. A hatch with a hinged opening at the top was raised, and his two comrades thrown inside. They couldn't keep their balance in their weakened state and staggered in, falling to the floor. The hatch was thrown back down, its base sliding into channels in the floor. A lock slid across, firmly holding it in place.

The three Barbarlars strode off laughing at their plight, knowing Jafar and his comrades were powerless. Jafar rushed to Boz first, whose arm was bound and tied to his chest.

"How is your wound?" he asked.

He turned Boz over onto his back and pulled out a tiny blade from the buckle of his compression suit. He slipped the blade into the binding and sliced it open until his one good arm came free. Boz groaned and seemed dazed.

"Alive," he replied.

Jafar cut Gur's restraints, too, and they both helped Boz sit up against the wall where Jafar had been moments before.

Both of them looked badly beaten. Blood had dried and congealed over their faces from injuries when they were first captured, and what looked like much more vigorous beatings since. He knew the only reason he had been spared such a beating was tradition, and that angered him. That Coskun would appear to stick to the tradition and rules of their ancestors so closely, and yet cheat in a fair contest in order to beat him.

"I am sorry we could not protect you," whispered Boz.

He was exhausted and barely able to get his words out. Jafar shook his head.

"No, there was nothing you could do. This was a trap that no manner of planning or skill could have wriggled out of, and I am sorry."

Boz nodded in gratitude, though Jafar didn't feel he deserved it. He picked up the plate with the remaining food and handed it to them to share.

"Even if we can escape, there is no way off this world without help from the Alliance. All we can do now is hope someone is foolish enough to come after us."

"But you ordered Commander Sarik to leave," Gur insisted.

"Yes, but there are others who would yet come for us."

* * *

Alita opened the door to Taylor's quarters aboard the Guam with a smile upon her face, but it was soon gone when she found an empty room. She tried his comms, but there was no answer, and so she set about looking for him. After trying several places, she strode into the armoury and found him sitting on one of the benches with the Morohta hammer across his lap.

"What are you doing with that?"

His right hand ran over the surface of the hammerhead as if he were studying it.

"We're going after big game. I figure I want to have the right tool for the job. A beast slayer."

"That thing is ridiculous."

"Yes, and it has got me out of more than a few tight spots, already."

"You cannot fight every battle single-handedly, you know that, right?"

He looked up to see genuine concern and worry in her face.

"And I don't, which is why I have come here. We need Jafar. We need his experience, strength, and leadership. Most of all, we need the Krys people, and few of their worlds will support us without him leading them."

"But you can't just go down there and seize power for yourself. A Human will never be accepted."

Taylor shrugged.

"I will do whatever I have to do."

She opened her mouth to speak but was interrupted by an open call over the loudspeakers.

"Colonel Taylor to the bridge."

He leapt to his feet and rushed forwards with the hammer in hand. He got to the bridge. Song was waiting for him.

"We are being hailed by a Barbarlar vessel. Commander Sarik has asked if you want to handle this."

"Sure, how many are out there?"

"Just one vessel, a small warship, but nothing of note."

"All right, put them on screen."

A Barbarlar appeared a few seconds later. He had the same primitive dress and hard faced look as the representative that had addressed Jafar.

"You bring a fleet where it is not welcome. I represent Lord Coskun of all the Krys peoples, and..."

"Of no people but his own," snapped Taylor.

The alien seemed shocked to have been interrupted.

"If your Lord held any power over the Krys people, then you would have a fleet here to protect this world. Instead, they stand here with me, a Human."

"You have no authority here, no matter how many traitors from our people support you. Advance any further, and you will be treated as an enemy."

Taylor ignored him and looked to the Captain.

"Target their weapon modules and engines."

She did not hesitate to relay the commands, and Taylor looked again at the Krys representative who still seemed utterly calm. He thought Taylor was calling his bluff, and that only made him smile.

"Ready to fire," replied Nichols.

Taylor looked into the eyes of the Barbarlar one last

time, but he could see he was not willing to concede a single thing.

"Fire!"

The gun batteries of the Guam opened up with one carefully targeted burst. They watched on another display as the impacts blew holes in the vessel. The Barbarlar was rocked in his seat, and the signal interrupted for a moment. The alien showed on screen before them once more, but he had nothing to say, so Taylor continued.

"Tell your master we are on our way. We come to negotiate, but any sign of force will result in an immediate carpet-bombing of every town and village we see. I will set this world on fire if you give me a reason to do so. There will be no glorious struggle, just genocide that I will have no pleasure nor doubt in dealing out."

He turned back to Song who seemed rather amazed and impressed at the same time.

"Advance towards the planet, and cut this fool off."

The Barbarlar said nothing before the transmission was terminated.

"That was an interesting form of diplomacy," she stated.

Taylor nodded.

"These Barbarlars will be beaten into submission or left for dead. It is their choice."

"You know we don't have the strength or firepower to do that?"

"Yes, but they don't know that."

They soared forwards and past the stricken enemy vessel en route to the planet. Song brought up camera views in front of them that projected deep into the world. Taylor was surprised at how underdeveloped it was. He had expected a primitive and simple world, not one that looked like nothing more than just wilderness.

"Why did we ever need these people? How useful can one planet be? Surely not worth all this risk?" Song asked.

"Is it worth fighting over? No, we can't afford the losses, but is it worth risking a few lives to gain an army, yes. Jafar knew that, he just didn't have the resources to pull it off. I should have had him wait until we returned from Yaxha, and maybe all this could have been avoided."

"Hindsight's a bitch. That's what you are always telling us," added Jones.

"Even so, I won't make the same mistake twice. I am taking the Guam's Marine detachment with me, and plenty more from the other vessels. Put me through to Sarik and Tuin."

Song was taken aback to hear them referred to so informally, and yet she did not question or doubt Taylor's ways.

The Commander and the Emperor appeared before them soon after.

"That was not how I expected you to handle this situation," started Sarik.

"Yeah, well surprise can be a powerful negotiating tool."

Jones smiled at the concept.

"I need two hundred of your Mechs to support me, and as many of your warriors Tuin."

"You have them," replied Sarik.

"We are at your disposal," Tuin added.

"Then follow my lead," he replied, and both parties ended the communication.

He turned back to Song. She was calmly awaiting his orders.

"You hold position, gun ports open. I want them to think we are willing to turn their home into a fireball."

"And if they attack you in force?"

"Rain down fire as much as you can, and get us out of there, but only on my signal."

She acknowledged the order and went on to carry out her duties.

"Let's go," Taylor said to Jones.

"Colonel!" Song called.

He stopped. She was standing at a display screen and frowning, as if trying to make sense of what she was seeing.

"What is it, Captain?"

"We are picking up signals from Lord Jafar's shuttle."

Taylor rushed to the console. She was looking at an overhead satellite view of a vast arena with the shuttle dwarfed near the centre.

"Why would they just leave it there? Not try to hide it or stop the signal?"

"Maybe they don't know how?"

Taylor smiled at Nichols and shook his head.

"No, it is a trophy, and likely a trap."

"So you will ignore it?"

"Nope, I'm gonna land right beside it."

The two Navy officers looked confused and waited for him to go on.

"They aren't afraid, and it is a statement of that fact."

"Doesn't that worry you?"

"Just stick to the plan, Captain, and cover our asses."

He left the bridge, and they returned to the docking bay and once again a scene that was becoming all too familiar. The ship's marines had been formed up, and all equipped as the Immortals now standing beside them. Most were veterans of the Yaxha mission, although there were plenty of new faces. Taylor strode up and down the line, trying to get a good look at every face of the men and women he was about to lead. He stopped to address them.

"I am sorry this had to come so soon. Such responsibility should have fallen on others after the exceptional service you gave on the Cholan homeworld. But that just isn't the way this has gone. It's on us, you and I. I fully expect and intend to fulfil this mission without firing a shot, but a show of force is necessary. Do not provoke these

Barbarlars. We may soon call them allies. Any questions?"

A young Lieutenant named Hartley spoke up. He had an artificial hand and a scarred face from burns Taylor knew he had suffered on Yaxha when storming the Emperor's Palace.

"Sir, are these really the sort of people we want to be fighting beside?"

Taylor smiled.

"Not really, but I am sure the enemy will feel far worse being in front of them than we will at their side."

A few laughed at his light heartedness.

"Our primary objective is to bring Jafar back alive so that he may continue his service as the leader of the aligned Krys worlds. Secondary objective is to get these savages on our side. Walk tall, be the intimidating sons of bitches I know you all are. Command respect, but show no intent of violence except in self-defence. Load up and move out!"

They rushed into the heavily armoured Stormer assault craft, and Alita took the pilot's seat of that carrying Taylor and their team. Mitch sat next to her so he could see the external display screens, as they soon passed through the atmosphere. She gasped at the sight of the first Ejdar.

"Commander Sarik warned us of those creatures, but I think he understated them a little."

"No shit," replied Taylor.

As they descended towards their location, they swooped

past one of the huge creatures and noted the Krys rider. Taylor was shaking his head.

"You know it's not so long ago that if you had told me something like that existed, I would have laughed and had you locked up for being insane."

"I am sorry to say that this is as much a shock to me as it is you."

Taylor smiled. It was the first time his comrades had felt like a fish out of water, as he had done since waking up in this new life. He was taking in all of the scenery now, just as Jafar had done, and coming to the same conclusions. It wasn't long until they saw the vast arena walls where the transponder message was hailing from. Alita cautiously checked the scanners and screens, expecting incoming fire any second, but it never came.

As they got overhead, and she slowed their descent for a smooth landing, they saw the shuttle near the centre of the open arena. She looked to Taylor for confirmation that he wanted her to land, and he nodded.

"I don't like this at all."

"Don't worry about it. We've faced far worse," replied Taylor.

Jones butted in. "It stinks, though. You don't enter a world with a small army, without any kind of opposition or questions being asked. Don't you think we are just being reeled into an ambush?"

"I thought about it, of course. But I also know the Krys,

and these are the most simple and primitive of them. It is important for their leaders to appear strong in front of their soldiers. If they will want anything out of this, it will be a personal contest."

"And still you came?" Alita asked.

"It's just a thought," he replied, shrugging as if it didn't bother him at all, "Put us down as planned."

She didn't look at all keen but still followed the order. They came in at a steep angle, and thrusters levelled them off at the last minute. They touched down just five metres away from Jafar's shuttle. Taylor was quick to hit the door release, and the murky foul air flowed in through the openings. He felt his nostrils burn and his eyes water slightly, but still he went forward.

He looked around in all directions for some sign of life, but all he could see were dozens of marines pouring out from each of the craft. Krys warriors were disembarking north of their position and Cholan to the right. He was surprised to see Emperor Tuin himself was leading the small force. His eyes met with the Cholan leader, and he nodded in respect of his efforts. Taylor stepped towards Jafar's shuttle. The ramp was lowered, and as he stepped up inside, he found it empty.

Where the hell is Jafar?

* * *

The ground shook slightly, and they heard the roar of engines overhead. Jafar knew it wasn't the Barbarlars, and he looked up to the hole to the surface above him. A Stormer passed by, and he caught just enough of a glimpse to recognise it.

"Taylor has come."

He heard a flurry of shouts coming from the guards down the corridor, and it brought a smile to his face.

"We are getting out of here," he said to the other two.

Footsteps rang out as one of the guards rushed to the entrance of the cell. It was the same repulsive guard he had communicated with before. He held a large two-handed axe in his hands.

"You hear that?" Jafar asked of the Barbarlar, "That is the sound of your doom."

"And yet here you stand, still a caged animal," the alien snapped.

Jafar smiled, stepping up to the bars of the cell, and that only infuriated the guard further. It was in this moment he noticed one of Boz's pistols slung from a primitive holster.

"You know your Lord is nothing more than a lying devious cheat?"

"The Barbarlar bore his teeth and took a step closer. The hulking guard stood as tall as Jafar and a little broader.

"Lord Coskun will have your tongue for such an insult."

Jafar stepped right up to the bars so that his face almost touched the thick branches.

"Why not take it now, or are you not up to the task?"

The Barbarlar's nostrils flared with anger, and he took a step up to the other side so that he was in arm's reach.

"I would gladly, if only my Lord would command it."

In a flash Jafar's arms were through the gaps in the cell branches and wrapped around the Barbarlar's neck. He wrenched him forward so that his head smashed into the hard and barbed surface, pinning his hands and weapon between them. With his left hand holding firm, he reached down for the pistol with his right and drew it to side of the alien's head. Jafar pulled the trigger before he could think or recover from the impact. The shot passed right through his skull and spewed blood out across the floor, and his body went limp.

Jafar pushed the body back so that it slumped far from the entrance. Boz and Gur were soon by his side.

"Taylor may have come for us, but that is no guarantee these barbarians will not try and kill us."

They nodded in agreement as he took aim at the hinges of the cell, shooting them off until the hatch collapsed onto the body of the fallen guard. Jafar handed the pistol to Boz, who could only use his one good arm. He then knelt beside the guard and smiled as he thought of the end he had met. He noticed the blade of the axe sticking out from between the body and the cell entrance and drew it out from his dead hands.

"Let's go."

* * *

Taylor looked around in all directions, making no attempt to take up any kind of defensive position, and that was making many of the marines restless. Then they heard a shriek that was shrill and echoed around the arena. Within seconds an Ejdar soared into view and landed twenty metres in front of him. The rider seemed to be assessing all those standing with him before lifting and blowing on a large horn. Trees all around the skirting wall of the arena began to rustle, and more than fifty of the creatures burst out into view, landing around them to encircle the combined forces at Taylor's disposal.

"What do we do?" Jones asked.

"Absolutely nothing." he said quietly.

There was an almost silent stand off as many of the Barbarlars leapt off their mounts and weighed up the foreigners. They looked highly suspicious and eager for blood.

"I bet they've never seen a Human before, let alone a Cholan," said Taylor.

"They don't look all that happy to see us."

"Would you, Jones? I remember the first time I saw an alien, and I wanted him dead, too."

A whole minute past as each side waited in a tense standoff. Taylor was expecting for one of them to come forward and announce themselves, but the silence went on so long he was starting to fear he had been wrong about them.

"This could turn ugly pretty quickly."

"Just wait, Jones, wait and see. I am betting whoever is in charge here will be curious enough to show their face and make a bit of a statement."

"Killing us all would be a statement," said Alita.

"That's not going to happen."

An even louder shriek rang out, and the huge Ejdar, Lord Coskun's mount that Jafar had encountered, swept in and landed halfway between his own troops and the encircled forces of Taylor. It was obvious he was the boss, and Taylor stepped forward out of the line towards him.

"This doesn't look good," said Jones.

Alita looked more uneasy than any of them as Taylor approached the huge winged beast and monstrous Barbarlar atop it.

"I am Colonel Mitch Taylor of..."

But he was rudely interrupted by the bellowing voice of the Barbarlar looming over him from a distance of two metres. Steam vented from the Ejdar. It bore its teeth and looked as if it wanted to eat him whole.

"You fired upon my ship. Explain yourself."

Taylor smiled and refused to be seen to be intimidated.

"Don't give me that honourable savage bullshit," he went on.

He strode forward and to the left side of the beast, reaching out to stroke its head. As he did, the Ejdar's jaw swung around as if to bite, but he had long seen it coming, pre-empting the beast by delivering a powerful hook with his right hand. It struck the creature on the nose. The sharp impact caused its head to crash to the ground, and it stumbled back slightly, throwing its rider. Coskun crashed to the ground beside Taylor, and the Ejdar retreated a few steps from them both.

Many of the Barbarlars raised their weapons, and Taylor's army did likewise, but he looked back at them with his hand raised.

"No!" he yelled.

He turned back to the Barbarlar whose ego had been badly bruised.

"Some beasts only understand a firm hand. Clearly, you need the same treatment."

"How dare you dishonour my leadership!" Coskun howled.

"I don't even know your name, and I don't care. I sent Lord Jafar here to negotiate peacefully. I gave you the carrot, and now I will give you the stick."

Coskun didn't understand the analogy, but Taylor's deviance only angered him further. He reached for the huge Bardiche slung over his back and appeared ready for a fight.

"If that's the way it has to be," stated Taylor.

He drew his Morohta hammer from his back, and it crackled with energy as it powered up.

"Stop!"

The voice was so loud it carried through the arena and caused everyone to turn and look. It was Jafar, with his two Krys warriors. The two were armed with pistol and axe, while Jafar stood empty handed. They had emerged from a stairway leading beneath the arena. Nobody said a word as he approached Taylor, but Coskun looked at him with both disgust and a little concern. Sarik rushed forward to Taylor's side as he approached.

"You knew my orders," Jafar said.

"And he followed them, but only so he could come back with a force strong enough to get this done the right way," replied Taylor.

Jafar nodded. "Thank you."

"Now if you don't mind, I have some business to attend to."

Taylor raised his weapon and turned back to Coskun.

"No," Jafar ordered firmly.

Taylor froze and couldn't believe what he had just heard.

"This savage imprisoned you."

"Yes, but look, he also commands the respect of his people. We need them, and you know it."

"Which is just what I am about to do."

Jafar shook his head.

"They will never accept you as their leader, and they will not except me if it is you who puts me in charge of them. I must do this myself."

Jafar sounded weary, but also determined.

"And if he kills you?"

"Have some faith in me, as I do you, my old friend. I have more than a little fight left in me yet."

"Did he not already defeat you in single combat?" Sarik asked.

Jafar looked back at the enemy leader to weigh him up once more.

"Yes, but not in a fair contest."

He reached out and grabbed hold of Taylor's hammer, though the Colonel didn't seem eager to release his hold.

"You sure about this?" he asked his oldest living friend.

Jafar nodded, and that was all Taylor needed to know. He let go, and Jafar strode forward to meet Coskun. Taylor and Sarik retreated to their own lines.

"Think he can win?"

"Yes," Sarik replied without hesitation.

Taylor sensed he would have said that no matter how he felt.

"You want to be humiliated a second time?" Coskun asked in a loud voice that carried far enough for most to hear.

Jafar stood still and weighed him up for a moment. He could see the same toxin poison device on Coskun's arm, and had no doubt he would try and use it again. Then he addressed the crowd himself.

"I call your Lord a cheat and a liar. He would not give me fair contest, but now I shall have it!"

Coskun laughed, but Jafar continued.

"I challenge your leadership, a fight in the ancient manner of our people. No weapons, no armour, nothing but what nature has given us!"

He threw his hammer back towards Taylor, and it slid to the ground a few metres from the Colonel's feet. Taylor didn't quite understand his reason, but noticing a glimmer of fear in Coskun's eyes, he knew Jafar was doing the right thing.

"Nothing can be a more fair contest, would you not agree?" Jafar called out to the crowd of Barbarlars.

Many of them began to roar and cheer with excitement at the prospect. Coskun knew he had no choice but to go along. He sighed and threw his Bardiche to the ground, unclipping his armour until both of them stood in nothing more than thin clothing. They stepped towards one another and well away from the equipment they had left behind. Each took up their fighting stances. Coskun was bouncing up and down on his feet as if to intimidate and show off his youthfulness, but Jafar advanced like the heavyweight he was. Taylor had once known him to be an agile fighter, but in his age he had become a tank.

Coskun jabbed quickly to Jafar's face as he neared. The

shock drove his head back a little, but it was not enough to stop him. He carried on forward and took another two to the face and seemingly showed no intent to parry or evade at all. He closed the distance and drove a deep uppercut into Coskun's stomach and followed it with another. The Barbarlar keeled forward, but Jafar hoisted him back upright and head butted him in the face. Coskun was thrown back, and blood poured from his face. He looked around at the crowd, his own people. They were silenced in shock. He knew he had to defeat Jafar or suffer humiliation for the rest of his life.

"You old fool," Coskun snapped.

He rushed forwards as if in a rage, but redirected and spun to deliver a backhand into the base of Jafar's spine. The impact jarred his spine and stunned him for a second, and in that opening, Coskun leapt onto his back with his arms wrapped around his throat in an attempt to choke him. The hold was too firm to break, so Jafar reached up and took told of Coskun's head and drove his thumbs into the Barbarlar's eyes. Coskun held on for as long as he could, but finally let out a cry of pain and his grip slipped. Jafar pulled him over his head and slammed him down back first in front of him.

Jafar raised his leg as if to stamp on Coskun, but he rolled out of the way and back to his feet. Once again they were both standing and opposing one another. Coskun looked desperate now. It was obvious to all that he did not have the strength to beat Jafar. He looked around and noticed his Bardiche just a few steps to his side. He quickly dashed and rolled across the ground and was up on his feet with it in both hands in a split second.

Nobody seemed bothered to try and intervene even though they all knew he was breaking the rules of the challenge. Jafar saw Taylor's hammer was a long way back, and even if he could make it, he didn't want to lesson his victory in the eyes of the Barbarlars. He glanced at Taylor and nodded. The Colonel knew exactly what he was saying. They needed the Barbarlars on board, and only an act of outstanding combat prowess was going to achieve it.

Coskun came at him now with a large horizontal swing that could cut any Krys in two. Jafar leapt back and voided the strike by millimetres. His enemy kept the blade in motion, swinging it about his head for the same strike, and still coming forward. Once again Jafar narrowly avoided it by maintaining the distance. But as the blade came around, Coskun took two large steps forward and brought it down for a massive vertical strike that Jafar could not back away from in time.

He did the only thing he could. He stepped forwards into the attack and crossed his forearms to parry the shaft of the Bardiche at the centre of the weapon, stopping it dead. Coskun could barely believe his eyes as Jafar took hold of the shaft and ripped it from his hands. As he did so, he took a pace back and pivoted the mighty weapon around at its centre point and struck Coskun in the face with the butt. The impact was so severe it dislodged his jaw. But Jafar did not stop there. He kept the blade in motion and took hold of the shaft as it past around his head and struck Coskun at the neck with the giant axe blade.

The razor sharp heavy blade cleaved through his neck with almost no resistance. The Barbarlar Lord's head was launched five metres through the air, rolling to a halt while his body stood upright. It toppled slowly like a falling tree before the triumphant Jafar.

Taylor couldn't believe his eyes. He didn't think Jafar still had it in him, and yet he should have know, for he himself knew how deadly the Krys Lords could be. He began to clap in respect and applause of his friend. Nobody made a sound, and Taylor's applause began to echo until the rest of his troops joined in. The Barbarlars joined in the sentiment as they struck the ground with the bases of their weapons. Jafar let them do so for a full two minutes as he got his breath back. His wound was once again throbbing, but he wouldn't show it.

"Silence!"

Jafar's deep roaring voice brought everyone's attention.

"I am Lord Jafar, leader of the aligned Krys worlds. I have defeated your master in fair trial and claim this world my own, and therefore, one of the aligned worlds. You fight for me now. Do you swear your allegiance?"

Nothing happened for almost a full minute as they

digested what was being asked of them. A few took a knee, lowering their weapons to the ground to submit to him. The rest of the Barbarlars in sight soon followed. It brought a smile to Taylor's face.

"That's how you take charge," said Jones.

"Fucking right," replied Taylor.

The marines began to cheer and whistle. Taylor could see it wasn't for what they would gain as an ally, but for Jafar's triumph, and the realisation they had completed the mission without a single loss of life or shot having been fired. Jafar strode triumphantly up to Taylor with Coskun's Bardiche still in one hand and the Barbarlar's blood dripping from its blade.

"The celebrations of a new Lord of Erzurum are a thing of legend, although I have never witnessed them myself. It would be an honour for you all to join me in these celebrations, and a great insult to them if you did not."

Taylor shrugged.

"Guess we're in then," he said and smiled.

CHAPTER SEVEN

Taylor threw back a huge drinking horn that was as large as his arm. The contents of which were far from tasty, but the effect of which was starting to dull his senses enough that he didn't mind. He sat back and looked up at the night sky. It was cooling quickly now, and fires had been lit around them for light and heat, a practice he had so often enjoyed in life, but rarely been able to experience.

"Did everyone in your age drink this heavily?" asked Lieutenant Hartley as he took a seat on a fallen tree beside Taylor. He too carried a drinking horn, but had barely touched its contents.

"Yeah, I guess so," he replied pleasantly.

"Does it help?"

Taylor's face turned from joy to concern, looking at the Lieutenant he could see he was still struggling with all they had to endure.

"I guess that's for you to decide, but if I can give you any advice, then it is to find all the joy you can in this life."

"How, and where?" he asked as if at a loss.

Taylor shook his head as if he had no answers himself, but then he looked up and saw Alita a few metres ahead. She was deep in conversation with Jones and several others of the Immortals. But as he gazed upon her, she locked eye contact and smiled back. It reminded him to heed his own message, and so pointed to the whole group who were merrily laughing and joking with one another.

"That's something. Doesn't matter how or where you find it, in a joke, in love, in a drink, in combat. You need something to enjoy."

"Combat as well?"

Taylor nodded and sighed.

"I'm not saying it's a walk in the park, and I know we have faced some terrifying things together, but you cannot deny it feels good to win. To vanquish an enemy, to complete a mission, and best a worthy foe."

"And you take pleasure in that? In death?"

Taylor nodded.

"If I didn't, I would have gone crazy by now."

The young officer fell silent for a moment, dwelling on those thoughts and feelings. Taylor took another drink.

"What does that make us, though?" he finally asked.

Taylor spilt some of the drink as he lowered the horn

and wiped it from his chin with his cuff. He knew he was seen as primitive compared to what humanity was today, and he simply didn't care.

"Good at our job."

A loud shriek rang out from an Ejdar, and they looked up. Coskun's impressive mount soared into view with its wings outstretched so that it was gliding smoothly through the air. It swooped past just twenty metres overhead. Taylor could see Jafar was riding it. The Barbarlars around them began to shout in a primitive language. It was clear they approved. Taylor just shook his head and took another drink. As he lowered it, he found Jones approaching.

"Who'd have thought it? It's like something out of a dream."

"I've seen enough crazy things and had enough surprises to last a lifetime that it just doesn't shock me anymore. I'm not sure what does surprise me now."

"I am sure there are things worse in this life that we are yet to face...Bolormaa for instance.

"You really know how to lift the mood," replied Taylor sarcastically.

They laughed, clashing their horns together and downing what they had left.

"More!" Taylor shouted as the festivities went on.

His vision was starting to blur, but he was feeling more relaxed than he had done in a long time. With Jafar, Jones, and Alita it was almost feeling like his old life again. He felt himself hit someone substantial; he had stumbled into a Barbarlar. Far from offended, the alien took his drinking horn from his hands and gave him a full one. Taylor took it gladly and smiled, as he let the night roll on and forget all his troubles.

* * *

Taylor awoke to find he was flat on his back and in a comfortable bed, the least likely position he expected to find himself in. He tried to get up, but his head was throbbing, and his body felt five times heavier than it should. With a grunt, he collapsed back down flat.

"What the fuck?"

He rolled and let his legs fall off the bed, using the motion to pull his body upright into a seated position on the side of the bed. He was in his quarters aboard the Guam and in nothing but his underwear. There was no sign of the clothing and armour he had been wearing the day before. He staggered to the wardrobe and dragged out the only other uniform he owned, pulling it on before making his way to the bridge. He swayed from one side to another and literally bounced off a few of the walls.

"Damn that's some brutal shit," he said as he got his footing.

He staggered onto the bridge. Jones was liaising with Song.

"Welcome back," said Jones.

"How?"

"How what, Colonel?" Song asked.

"How are you not hit by this?" he asked Jones.

The Lieutenant laughed in response.

"Because the rest of us took a taste of the Barbarlar liquor out of friendship. I think you nearly drank the bar dry."

Taylor shook his head.

"What is it with your generation and a need to consume volumes of intoxicating substances that would numb the most robust of creatures?"

He had no answer for it, but his aching head made him wonder the same.

"Where are we?"

"We have just made the jump to Ares."

Oh, shit!

A few seconds later a comms channel was opened, and the President appeared.

"Mr President," Song acknowledged.

Oh, no, he thought.

"Colonel Taylor, is he aboard?" Isaacs asked.

Taylor staggered into view.

"Just about still alive," he replied, trying to make light of it all.

"Once again you have plucked victory from disaster, Colonel!"

His sharp tone and loud volume reverberated through Taylor's eardrums and only served to hurt him more. He nodded a few times in agreement before sitting back against one of the bridge consoles to rest his weary body.

"I can see you need your rest, Colonel. Please do not let me keep you from your bed. Report at 0900 to me personally aboard Ares 4. The Alliance is keen to see their hero, and we will be sure to parade him appropriately."

"Great," muttered Taylor.

The signal ended, and Song looked at him accusingly.

"Colonel, you just blew off the most powerful person in the Alliance."

"Yeah? Didn't seem all that bad to me."

"This is his way, Captain," added Jones.

"What way?"

"A blatant disregard for authority. Pig headedness. He is everything a superior officer hates, and everything he needs all at once. Every day of his history is like that. Nobody likes it, but everyone has to accept him eventually."

"Thanks," replied Taylor.

He staggered off the bridge and back to his room. He opened the door and found Alita waiting for him inside. She was lying on his bed wearing nothing but her panties, yet he collapsed beside her and barely recognised her presence.

"It seems we have found something that can beat the mighty Colonel Taylor," she joked.

"That stuff's hardcore. Be sure to find some more. Next time I want to drink to forget, it is sure to do the trick," he replied, as he fell into a semi dream like state, responding in muted tones as she went on.

"Is that what you do, drink to forget all the things you have seen, and the people you have lost?"

"Yes," he mumbled.

"I hope I mean that much to you some day."

"What?" he mumbled again.

Though he was too tired to wait for the response.

"I love you," she added.

But he had already slipped into a deep sleep.

* * *

The next time Taylor awoke he found himself fresh and ready to run. Within an hour of waking, he was aboard the Ares station to meet with the President. He expected some offer of medals or public celebration, but what he got was not what he was expecting or wanting at all. He stepped into the operations room. Isaacs and many other high-ranking officers were watching a corny recruitment video that featured many photos and videos of him and his Immortals. The video ended with a triumphantly posed photo of him standing on top of a craggy mountaintop. The narration ended - 'Sign up today and become a hero of the Alliance.'

He shook his head at both the slogan, and the fact he knew the photo had been digitally mocked up. It was false advertising at best, and painfully misleading.

"Do you like it, Colonel?" asked the President.

From the proud and happy face of Isaacs, this advertising campaign was his new baby. Taylor barely knew how to respond, so he simply shrugged.

"Oh, come on, Colonel. You are a hero. There is no shame in making that news."

"This isn't news. It's promising people something they will likely never know. You're making out that it's some kind of walk in the park or video game. This is war, and it isn't pretty. You show a load of images of people posing in armour and training in safe environments. Where is the war, the death, the loss, the hardship?"

"We're trying to recruit people, not send them running in fear."

Taylor shook his head.

"Yeah, I got that," he replied sarcastically.

The President pressed a few keys and brought up the view outside the station where the battered fleets of the Alliance were still undergoing repairs.

"You see that, Colonel?"

He nodded and Isaacs went on.

"That is the core of our fleet. Modest compared to what we must face, and still in need of months of refits and repairs. The Alliance is weak in ships and other combat vehicles and equipment, but we are strong in manpower. We need to leverage that manpower."

Taylor was starting to come over. He didn't like being used to cheat and deceive people, but understood the President was doing it for the right reasons.

"Tell me, Colonel, when you signed up, back in the day, were you recruited on the basis of having to fight a war, or was it the excitement and adventure that drew you in?"

"Was a little different. There were no alien races back then, and not really any wars either."

"And if there were, would that have put you off?"

He didn't even know anymore. War was all he did know.

"I guess not."

Isaacs played the advert once again. Taylor cringed even further as he saw footage from the beginning that he had missed first time around. Some was genuine and unaltered, such as him in training scenarios when he first drilled and prepared those who now called themselves Immortals. He had no idea he was even being filmed, but from the footage there must have been drones tracking his actions most of the time.

"You had these cameras on me all this time?"

Isaacs seemed uneasy and stuttered, trying to respond while Taylor waited for an explanation.

"You have to understand, Colonel, we had no idea how it would turn out. Whether you could be trusted, how you would react. Even if the historical documentation of your character and victories were true, we had little idea of what the passage of time and the awakening in a new time would do to your mind. We needed to keep check on you, and you know you would do the same with any valuable asset you knew little about."

Taylor relaxed as he tried to get his head around it. For once Isaacs was right, though he still didn't like it.

"This is just the beginning, Colonel. We are making you the face of resistance. Of hope."

He could already sense there was something coming he wasn't going to like.

"I want you to become the public face of this war."

He spun around to access his console and pressed a few keys until a poster was displayed before them with an old officer. He had a massive moustache and a slogan reading 'Britons, I want you. Join your country's army!' Taylor had seen it before, but he wasn't familiar with its history.

"Lord Kitchener," added Isaacs, "One of the greatest examples of military recruitment in wartime the Human race has ever known; an old soldier and hero of multiple wars. The people of his nation rallied to the call of a hero and enthusiastically signed up to fight."

"Doesn't look like I have much choice. You've already done this."

"No, Taylor. We live in a different age to Kitchener, even you did. A more advanced age of integrated communication. I want you to go live on the news for interviews. To tours of schools and cities, rally the people through a public tour that can be followed by every means of social media at our disposal. You'll have young men and women signing up in the millions.

Taylor shook his head.

"Use my image, fake some videos, I don't care all that much, but I will not be a puppet paraded around like some circus act. I have been there and experienced it firsthand. However positive an effect you might think it will have, the result will be very different. Those were dark days."

A Naval commander nearby piped up.

"All the wars you have lived through and you call those dark days?"

Taylor nodded with hesitation.

"To have the support of a people when at war is far preferable to being hated by your own people in peace."

Isaacs saw he had struck a nerve and stood up with outstretched hands to intervene.

"Okay, okay, I think we understand one another. Please take a seat, Colonel."

"I'd rather not. There is much to be done, if you are finished?"

Isaacs nodded.

"Okay, Colonel, and thank you for your understanding. This will help our cause more than any action you can carry out singlehandedly."

He thought about it and turned to leave but stopped

himself.

"I'll do one piece for you. One sketch that you can use for recruitment."

Isaacs' eyes lit up with excitement.

"But no interview, just me and a camera. I choose my words, and you don't edit or screw with them. When it's done, you can take it or leave it."

"That would be extremely helpful, thank you."

Taylor couldn't believe how much the President was pandering and grovelling to him. It felt as though he could just reach out and take the President's seat of power without a fight. That thought worried him. He never wanted that power, but he feared what others might do if they saw him as a threat to what they have. Too many times before his own superiors had betrayed him.

"You know I am just a fighting man?"

The President looked confused, so he went on.

"I never want political office or any of that. Sometimes I do the craziest of things, but only for the right reasons. I am no threat to you, you understand that, right?"

Isaacs looked both a little reassured and uncertain all at the same time.

"Give me an hour, and I'll be back to give you your recording."

"Thank you, Colonel."

As he exited the room, he found Jones leaning against a wall outside waiting for him. The Lieutenant quickly jumped to his side and carried on as he walked. He waited for Taylor to speak, but when nothing came, he started asking the questions.

"What are our orders?"

Taylor shook his head. "We don't have any."

"Then what are we to do?"

"That's what I am about to find out."

It was a cryptic response, but Jones knew he wasn't going to get any more information, so he followed the Colonel as he weaved from one corridor and floor to another. They reached the ambassadorial quarters and strode up to Irala's room. Before he could even press the buzzer, the door slid open as if he were expected.

They stepped in to the rather spacious quarters. It was stark, with no decoration and little of anything at all beyond a bed and a stool. Irala was sitting upon the stool as if in a meditative state.

"You want to know how to kill Bolormaa?" Irala asked. He opened his eyes but did not move.

"How did you guess?"

"Because you are, as your people say, like a dog with a bone."

Taylor smiled in response, for he couldn't deny it.

"What is he talking about?" Jones asked.

"Some way of killing the creature that we don't know. In the aftermath of the Cholan attack, he mentioned it. I've not stopped thinking about it since, but this is the first spare moment I have had to pursue it. Hence the sentiment."

Irala remained sitting silently atop his stool, as if waiting for another question.

"What are you even doing in here?" Taylor asked, "Just sitting about, what is it that you do?"

"I think," he replied calmly.

"Think? With all the things we need to do to prepare for this war."

"When you have lived as long as I have, you soon begin to appreciate the moments when we may sit back for hours or even days at a time and contemplate all the facts. Other races see or believe that we can predict the future, but as I told you a long time ago, we are simply thorough in our calculations in all matters in life. When you can afford the time to do nothing, but piece together all the knowledge and information you have, you may come to conclusions that might otherwise be missed by those who rush in."

"What are you implying?" Taylor asked while still smiling.

"You haven't changed a bit, have you?" asked Jones.

Taylor shrugged.

"Don't see why I ever should."

"Well, Irala, what is it you have? What do you know that the rest of us don't?"

"You know that Bolormaa is said to be unkillable? And you know firsthand from meeting one of her spawn that the reputation could indeed be fact?"

"Yeah, but I can't see that bastard making it out of that. Ganbaatar went down with that bomb. I saw him fall into darkness."

"Did you see him die?"

Taylor shook his head.

"Then you know nothing. Ganbaatar has survived more than you can ever imagine. Show me his head, and only then will I believe he is dead."

"Okay. Let's believe she is as unkillable as you say, then you know a way of killing these bastards, so tell us."

Irala took a deep breath.

"What I am about to tell you is considered to be little more than myth by many of my people."

Taylor and Jones said nothing, waiting in suspense for him to continue.

"There is a weapon that was said to be in the possession of our people. A weapon forged by Bolormaa's birth mother herself."

Taylor couldn't wait any longer as Irala spoke so slowly.

"What kind of weapon?"

"A spear."

But Taylor waited patiently now for him explain.

"A weapon so uniquely powerful it could penetrate any substance known in the universe. To my people it is known as the Pauri Tao, but they are known to have called it Tam Ir, or Tamir. I am not sure their people believe in its existence any more than most of my people do."

"But you believe in it, don't you? Or you wouldn't have baited me with the very idea?"

Irala nodded.

"Many of my people would scorn me for ever having told you, but there are a few who still believe."

"Where is it?" Jones asked impatiently.

Irala frowned a little, and Taylor could see this was the sticking point.

"Rumoured to be buried deep below the surface of our homeworld."

"Onesaka?"

Irala shook his head.

"No, Jones, he means the one before the Krys invasion, the planet that was obliterated by them. Is it not just a wasteland now?"

"Yes it is."

"Then why haven't you been back there to recover this weapon?"

"For too long the Krys ensured we never could, and as time has passed, it has fallen from legend to myth, and all but forgotten. Too few of us still believe to pursue it for ourselves, and the risk the Morohta now present means we cannot contemplate such a venture. Not without help."

Taylor paced back and forth, thinking about the prospect of such a powerful weapon.

"Surely this is just a fairytale that you tell kids?" Jones

asked, "Are you not familiar with the sword Excalibur?"

"I know more about Human culture than you could ever expect to learn in the years you have in this life."

"Then you know every culture has some bullshit fairy tale of a magical weapon that can do all kinds of amazing things? Why would your story be any more believable? If we were to go looking for Excalibur, we would be considered insane, probably locked up. What possible reason do you have to believe this Tamir thing exists?"

Both looked to him for some kind of answer, but he didn't seem willing to give up anything more.

"Come on, my old friend," Taylor pleaded, "You cannot expect us to buy into such a story and act upon it without a little more reason to believe it. You clearly do, and passionately so. Tell us why, make us believe as you do."

He did not respond.

"Come on." He beckoned to Jones and headed for the door.

"Okay," said Irala.

Both of them stopped and listened intently.

"My grandfather, Tane Mahuta, was alive when my people fought the Morohta. When I was young, he was one of the few surviving from that war. Even then, it was fading from memory for my people. He was there the day one of our people took up the Pauri Tao. He seized it from Bolormaa in single combat, the great hero Rua. He inflicted a wound upon the beast with the weapon, but was himself dealt a mortal wound."

"And you believe the story your grandfather told you?"

"Yes, Lieutenant Jones, I would have no reason not to."

"So what happened to the weapon?" asked Taylor.

"It was buried deep within the surface of our planet. Only a handful knew of its existence and location; to all others it was nothing more than a myth. Our council of leaders believed the very existence of such a weapon would act as a deterrent to Bolormaa."

"Did it?"

"Of a sort. None of our people ever saw Bolormaa with their own eyes again. Many believed she was too terrified to ever come near the weapon."

"Why not just destroy the planet?" asked Jones, "I am sure she had the means."

"Because the Pauri Tao is sacred to her. It was a great insult to have lost it. Why her terrible war stopped we may never know. But my grandfather believed that had the war lasted for even a few more weeks, the weapon would have been discovered. All those who knew of its presence were tortured and eventually killed, but no one ever revealed its location."

"All but your grandfather?"

"None knew that he was there that day. He had left his post in assistance of Rua, and for that he was disgraced. Nobody ever believed his story."

"Except you?" asked Jones.

Irala nodded once again.

"And you still believe them?" asked Taylor.

"Nothing would give me cause to doubt."

"And you believe we will need this weapon if we are to defeat Bolormaa."

"Yes, I do."

Taylor paced back for forth again as he tried to make sense of it all.

"You take this to the President and he will call you insane."

"Wouldn't be the first time, Jones."

"What are you going to do?"

* * *

Two days had passed as Taylor had wandered the station in a daze, thinking about Irala's story. Every time he thought how insane it sounded, he remembered his encounter with Ganbaatar. He knew they needed something more than what they were able to assemble. He finally found himself outside Irala's door once again. The door opened. Jones was sitting inside the room with the Councillor.

"Well, Colonel, have you made up your mind?" Irala asked.

Taylor rubbed his chin and wiped his brow, still trying to decide whether to believe the story. He looked into

Irala's eyes, recalling everything they had been through together, and realised it was enough.

"There is a whole lot of work to be done, and there ain't much we can do at this stage. A small elite team, this is exactly the kind of mission we were made for."

"It's not for you to decide though, is it?"

"I say it is, Jones."

"You know you have a real problem with authority?"

Taylor smiled.

"You always think you know better. Someday it's going to go horribly wrong."

"It has many times. I never said I always made the right decisions or got everything right, but I go with my heart and my gut, and it's gotten us a long way so far."

"It's hard to refute that, but you're talking about asking the Alliance to authorise a mission to chase after a magical spear that is what, thousands of years old?"

"Yeah, I guess I am. Come with me."

He headed to the door.

"Where are you going?"

"To make this happen, Irala, and you are coming with us. If you expect us to put our asses on the line for this story of yours, then you better be willing to risk just as much."

He got up off his chair and followed the two officers to Isaacs' operations room.

"Colonel Taylor, back so soon?"

"I needed a job to do, and I have found one."

Isaacs seemed surprised.

"Please, enlighten us."

Taylor gestured towards Irala to come forward, and they once again heard the farfetched story from the Aranui Councillor. When he finished, the room was held in a tense silence. Many didn't know whether to laugh or not, and Taylor could see every single one of them doubted the significance or even truth of it all.

"It is a wonderful story, Councillor, but how does it help us?" the President asked.

Taylor leapt forward to say his piece.

"We need this weapon because it won't be a mighty weapon or ship that will kill Bolormaa and her cursed offspring. It will be a man."

"I think we are a little past single combat, Colonel. This is not the middle ages," replied the Commander who had questioned him once before.

"Really? That's what I was told in my day, and yet it was me who killed Lord Erdogan, with my own hands and the weapons I carried in them!"

"Hundreds of years ago," Isaacs intervened, "Now we have ships like the Nakbe that could end this monster, and whatever ship she travels in, in a single shot."

"You think wonder weapons are anything new? The Katil could destroy entire planets."

"I just don't know what you want from me. You are

both coming to me with stories long in our past that seem to have little relevance, if any, to our current situation."

Taylor took a deep breath, desperately trying to think of some way of convincing them.

"I know this sounds crazy, but maybe a little crazy is what we need. Give me a few ships, and let me search for this weapon. I am not even sure myself if it is real, but if there is even a remote chance of getting our hands on such a game-changer, you have to let me go after it."

The President sighed and shook his head, but he looked around and many of the officers seemed okay with the idea. Taylor could only imagine they would be glad to be rid of him.

"You can take the vessels you went to Yaxha with, but not a single other one. We just cannot afford them."

"That's all I need."

"When will you depart?"

"No time like the now. Mr President, keep recruiting, keep building ships, and keep developing weapons. Do not pause the war effort for anything. Whether I find this weapon or not, you will see me again."

Taylor and Jones left the room.

"Think any of them believe in this spear?"

Taylor shook his head. "Nope, Jones, but what does it matter?"

"A spear? Like the Spear of Destiny?" Jones asked rhetorically.

"Let's hope it's foundation in reality is a little more plausible."

CHAPTER EIGHT

Taylor looked at his console. A week had passed, and they were still in sight of Ares 4. He was getting restless, but he knew the time had come. He watched Song's shuttle depart the station en route to their modest fleet. He observed Nichols staring at the Captain's chair that he coveted so much.

"You want it, don't you?"

Nichols nodded.

"I loved Commander Cohen."

"And now we've got two captains on one ship."

"Yes," he sighed.

"You understand I never wanted that scenario? You might feel that being executive officer with your rank is somehow degrading, but all you need to know is that we must all give our best. We need top people for the job, and

193

if that means I have more captains than ensigns, more NCOs than privates, so be it. This is war, Captain. Men and women come and go on a daily basis. Field commissions can see you rise quicker than you ever thought possible, and to fall just as quickly. Don't let pride get in the way. We are all in this together."

"Aye, aye, Sir."

Taylor could see he wasn't totally convinced. Song was the better officer, and that had been clear from the start, but he never wanted to tell Nichols as such. He left the bridge without another word to go and greet the Captain, leaving Nichols to continue carrying out last minute preparations.

When the shuttle landed and the door opened, Song stepped out with just two of her staff.

"Where is Irala?" Taylor asked without even offering a greeting.

"The Councillor has asked me to pass on his apologies that he will not be joining us in this mission, though he has once again supplied us with one of his vessels to act as a gateway for our journey," replied Song as she strode past and headed for the bridge.

Taylor carried on at her side.

"So this is it? It's a purely Human operation?"

"Commander Sarik has provided a platoon of his best Krys warriors to assist you."

One platoon, amazing!

"Doesn't it strike you as a little odd that no one is willing to get behind this operation?"

"Not really. It's a mission with a very low probability of success. A wild goose chase, if you ask me. Were it not for your insistence, it would not even go ahead. You've got some leeway here, Colonel, but we are going to need to see some results quickly, or I have my orders to return to Ares 4."

"You don't even believe in this?"

"It doesn't matter what I believe. It only matters what we can achieve. I am with you on this, Colonel. I trust you, but you cannot deny this sounds more than a little crazy; mystical weapons with magic powers that haven't been seen in thousands of years. Be careful. People believe in you, but their patience has a limit."

Taylor sighed, knowing it was true.

They got to the bridge where Irala was projected before them.

"Guess your belief in this isn't quite as strong as you let on," said Taylor.

There was a little anger in his voice, and he could not deny it. His old friend had sold him on the idea of this mission, and he was not impressed he did not have the courage of his convictions to go through with it.

"We're going to your former homeworld, and yet you aren't coming along? Wasn't this your dream?"

Irala looked a little sheepish and embarrassed.

"My people will not let me go. We made a pact a long time ago that we would not return to those lands. Many still believe they are cursed."

"But you would happily risk our lives in such as endeavour?"

"You have to understand our position, Colonel. Every one of us is lost is like losing five million of yours. It is not that we are more important, just that there are so few of us left. As ever, I will provide you with all the assistance I can, but Aranui lives must be protected, or we will soon be extinct."

Taylor knew he wasn't going to get anywhere.

"One last thing."

"Yes?"

"The Morohta, do they know the location of this weapon?"

Irala shook his head.

"If they knew, they would have long since recovered it. As far as they are concerned, it could be hidden anywhere in the universe. Even if they suspected it of being on our former homeworld, they would never find it."

"This homeworld, what is it called?"

Irala looked down at Song as if he didn't want to answer.

"What's the deal?"

"It is a very sore subject for our people, Colonel, and we long since vowed to never speak its name again."

"That's a hell of a way to honour and remember what

you lost."

"You don't know what we went through in the Krys wars."

"I think I've got a pretty good idea," snapped Taylor, "You want us to go looking for this weapon, then you better start being more upfront with the facts."

Irala hesitated but then answered.

"I had in my possession an encrypted data card, as well as a locator beacon and clues as to the location of the weapon. I have entrusted Commander Song to make sure they reach you."

Taylor glanced at Song.

"You will find them in your quarters."

"Everything I ever knew about the weapon is contained in that box, and every clue I have to finding it. You are about to embark on a journey I have waited my entire life for..."

There was a pause as Irala clearly fought his own conscience.

"The planet is called Moana. Once eighty percent of the world was covered in luscious oceans, but even now is believed to still be a toxic wasteland."

"Anything else you want to tell me?"

"If Bolormaa has any inclination we might be searching for the Pauri Tao, and has any means to reach you, she will do everything in her power to stop you."

"But we closed off their means of navigation?" Jones

joined in.

"To their main fleets, that is indeed true, but do not forget Kepler 186, Lieutenant. Whatever you discovered there, it had been buried and waiting a long time for some sign of life to stumble across it."

"Got it," replied Taylor.

"Then that is all I have to offer. Good luck, Colonel."

Taylor acknowledged and turned to Song.

"Let's get rolling."

"It will take us three jumps to safely reach Moana, and even then I would have us enter space forty kilometres from the world so that we may evaluate the situation and make a safe approach."

"Three jumps?"

"The Councillor tells me the Aranui navigation mapping of the area is long out of date. We cannot jump safely in one single trip. We must gain data as we draw nearer."

None of that meant much to Taylor, but he accepted it.

"I'll be in my quarters going over this mysterious data Irala has given me."

"Do you want to be on the bridge when we arrive at Moana, Colonel?"

"If there is trouble, yes. Otherwise just notify me when you are ready for us to go down to the surface."

He gestured for Jones to follow him and left to go to his quarters. They entered to find Alita sitting at his small desk. A pistol was on the table beside a small box of

Aranui construction.

"Trying to break the lock?"

"Just keeping guard, Mitch. I had orders from Irala to ensure nobody got their hands on this box but you."

Taylor paced up to the table and just stared at the box for a few moments. It was typical sleek Aranui design. There were marks and scuffs. Despite it being spotlessly clean it look rather old.

"He really believes in this, doesn't he?"

"I don't doubt that, Jones. He wouldn't send us into trouble without believing it."

"But do you?"

Taylor shrugged at Alita's question. It was as honest an answer as he could give.

"Then why take us out there?"

"Honestly? Because right now we've got nothing else to do, and I've seen enough unbelievable shit to give this a shot. When everything you ever thought was true gets turned on its head, you have to start giving the most unbelievable and unlikely of stories a chance."

"For a man with no faith in religion that is curious," added Jones.

"Hey, if a God turned up and showed me his skills, I'd believe. I didn't believe in aliens either, but when they're standing in front of you and trying to blow your head off, it makes a believer of you."

He took a step closer to the box. They both watched

him intently and with some suspicion and intrigue.

"How the hell am I supposed to get into this thing?"

He laid his hand on the surface and around the sides of the box that was less than half a metre square, but there appeared to be no sign of any lock, clasp, or hinges. His hand reached the top, and he stretched his palm out flat. The top of the box began to glow, and a green border lit up tracing the shape of his hand. The top then separated into four parts and retracted into the sides to reveal its contents.

"Guess it likes you," Alita smiled.

"You already tried to get in?" Jones asked.

"Of course I did. Entrusted with one of the universes secrets. Of course I wanted to know what was inside."

He pulled out what looked like a solid steel baseball, and as he took hold of it, a projection of Irala sprung up before him. It was not as clear as usual and quite transparent.

"Colonel Taylor. I have programmed this device with my knowledge. You may ask it anything you like. It has only a simple function to analyse and think, but can access a wealth of data that may help you. Place this inside the Guardian when you are nearby, and it will help you greatly. Everything in this box has been programmed to self-destruct should it ever be more than one kilometre from your presence, so please keep it close at all times."

The projection ended.

"Well that was weird," he muttered.

He reached in and pulled out a small datapad of Human construction, the type that connected to the forearms of their suits. It lit up as he touched it. It was a map of a world he did not recognise.

"He couldn't just have sent this data to your own console?"

Taylor shook his head. "Irala is keeping this off the grid. It is not connected by any means to other devices or networks. This is for our eyes only."

"You know one thing no one has considered in all this?"

They waited for Jones to go on.

"...This is a spear. It's not a ship, a gun, but a spear. It might be the most powerful spear the universe has ever known, if it does indeed exist. But it is still just a spear. Someone has to get close enough to Bolormaa to use it, and we haven't managed that yet, and I am not sure anyone would be crazy enough to want to."

"Yeah, well, we'll cross that bridge when we come to it."

"The Colonel is the master of single combat, remember," added Alita.

"Yes, I am well aware of his file."

"Leave me with this. I need to think," said Taylor.

They both got up and left without another word. But as they exited the room, they looked at one another with concern.

"Think this is a wild goose chase?"

"Maybe, Alita, maybe."

"You know what Irala told me when he gave me the box?"

Jones shrugged.

"To look after Taylor. He said, for all that Mitch is, he is still just a man, and can be killed as easily as you or I."

"I think history would tell us otherwise."

"He said, without good people by his side, Taylor is little more than one good warrior in a vast battle. He said he would need us as much as we need him."

***

Taylor felt each of the jumps they made as he went through the information Irala had sent him. There was surprisingly little. Just a map and locator device, as well as some riddles of how to access the chamber that was described.

"Why on earth did he never come for it himself?"

Then he began to dwell on Jones' words.

What use is such a powerful weapon if it cannot be brought to bear? It must have seemed a useless relic when hordes of Krys invaded.

Hours had passed when Song called him to the bridge. He arrived to see they were in orbit with the planet. It was a stark, dusty world. Large mountain ranges and canyons formed what used to be vast oceans. They now just contained the murky remnants of the vast waterways that would have made the planet a luscious world, more akin to Taylor's favourite parts of Earth.

"What did the Krys do here?" asked Jones.

Taylor looked to Babacan for answers, though he knew it was well before his day.

"They were dark days for my people. Once considered one of our greatest triumphs, but now a history we try to forget."

"Your ancestors fought so hard to take Earth, a paradise according to your myths and legends, and yet you probably had the chance of something just like it here. Why destroy that?"

Babacan had no answers, but Taylor could already imagine why. He thought back to the sadistic Lord Demiran, who would have Earth destroyed rather than see a single Human live upon it.

"I am picking up some signs of life down there," said Nichols.

"What?" Taylor demanded.

"They...they are not Aranui."

"The Morohta, they must have got here ahead of us..." suggested Jones.

"No...they are Krys."

"Show me!" Taylor ordered sharply, as he tried to wrap his head around the reason for them being there.

A screen flashed up, and a bird's eye view revealed a small town. It was certainly of Krys construction, and they could see Krys and their vehicles going about their daily business.

"Looks like a settlers village," said Jones.

"What?"

"You know, like those old Wild West movies."

"You think that's what this is?"

Babacan stepped up beside Taylor for a better look. His eyes opened wide as he understood. There were symbols on the rooftops that he obviously recognised.

"Well, who are they?" Taylor asked.

"Cingenes," he replied confidently, if a little surprised.

"What?"

"They are a nomadic cult that come from three of our worlds. They serve merely for the benefit of travel. That is their pay."

"So what, they just take up on any world they are taken to?" asked Jones.

"Yes. They are a strange people. Simple, devious, and not to be trusted."

"Why would they come here?"

Babacan shook his head and shrugged.

"How long have they been here?"

"This world was uninhabitable for a long time," replied Song.

"Yes, but they are also hardened people. Judging by what they have built here, thirty years, maybe longer," replied Babacan.

"But why?"

"Why doesn't matter right now, Jones. Are they dangerous?"

"Yes. They will attack any potential threat they see. They are simple, but tough people. They are also deeply religious and believe they are above all others."

"Are they anywhere near our target? Can't we just avoid them altogether? There can only be a few hundred by the looks."

Taylor looked down at the console Irala had given him and shook his head.

"No, Commander, they have settled over the remnants of the capitol city, right where we are heading."

"How do they feel about other races, Babacan?" Jones asked.

"They are not kind towards them."

Taylor sighed. "Will they accept any kind of authority?"

"A Krys Officer or Lord with enough troops at his back, yes."

"That's helpful."

The bridge fell silent, but Taylor looked at Babacan with a smile.

"Fancy playing a Krys Lord?"

* * *

"Think they have ever seen a Human before?" Jones

looked worried as he asked.

Taylor looked to Babacan. His armour had been hastily decorated and adorned with precious metals by the ship's engineers.

"I doubt it," he replied. He looked less than comfortable with the whole situation.

Half of the craft was filled with Krys warriors from the platoon Sarik had provided. Taylor couldn't help but feel safe amongst them with his Immortals in support.

"This is not going to work."

"You said yourself these are simple folk. We put on a good enough show, and we'll be fine. It's called a bluff."

Babacan shook his head.

"I have no idea how to act like a Lord."

"Yeah? Just walk like an asshole, and talk like you own everything and everyone, and you'll be fine."

Jones couldn't help but laugh. "The feudal Lords I descended from would be turning in their graves."

"I knew your family had some history, but not that much?"

"Oh, there was land and title back in my family."

"Yeah? What happened?" Alita asked.

"War," he replied solemnly.

The light tone was killed just as quickly as Jones had created it, as they all knew how that felt. Taylor turned his attention back to Alita at the helm.

"Stick to plan, keep it calm. We aren't trying to surprise

them here."

"Still doesn't feel right going in with no cover at all."

"We've got cover. Don't you worry!"

They came in to land just fifty metres away from the edge of the small town. Ten Stormers put down, and Taylor was first out of the door. He signalled for the others to join him, and Babacan stepped out without weapon in hand and stood like a statue as if awaiting some kind of reception. The town had the appearance of having been made from prefabricated quick build structures, thinner and weaker than anything normally seen from the Krys. More than twenty Krys approached. None wore armour, but all had on thick quilted clothing and carried typical Krys issue pulse cannons.

"Guess they aren't that primitive," whispered Jones.

They approached confidently and brashly, as if with no concern at all. Several had their guns slung on their shoulders or held at their side. They seemed to perceive the newcomers as no threat at all.

"They seem awfully confident."

"Never mistake cockiness for confidence, Jones," replied Taylor.

The group of Cingenes stopped ten metres in front of them, appearing to be weighing them up and waiting for some introduction. Taylor wanted to handle them himself, but he knew he could not.

"I present to you Lord Babacan!" Taylor announced.

He stepped aside and let his Krys friend pass through into the opening between both sides.

"We are here on a mission that is not of your concern. We come to you out of respect before we go about our business!"

One of the Cingenes stepped forward. He looked a little older than most there, but was dressed the same as all the others.

"So these are the Humans, Lord Babacan? They do not look like much!"

"Looks can be deceiving. Let us not forget that it was a Human who felled the mighty Lord Erdogan!"

"Is that one among you?"

Taylor smirked a little. It was an absurd question to ask if you knew what a Human's lifespan was, and yet, in this case the answer was the most unlikely. Babacan looked to Taylor who subtly shook his head.

"I count the slayer of Erdogan amongst my friends, but he would not concern himself with a trivial mission such as this."

"What is your purpose here?"

"None of his business," Taylor said quietly.

"You need not know what our business is, only that our stay will be short," replied Babacan.

Nice one, Taylor thought.

The Cingene passed his rifle to the one standing next to him and approached.

"A Krys Lord amongst us. It would be an honour if you would join us while your people do whatever they need to do."

Babacan looked uncertain and to Taylor for answers, both knowing they had to make a response if they wanted to try and keep things civil.

"I accept," he replied to the Cingene, looking at Taylor.

"I will keep my personal guard. You may get to work."

Taylor bowed slightly as Babacan signalled for the eight Krys warriors he had with him to go forward.

"I am Benli, and I rule this world, the four hundred and eighteen Krys who live here," said the Cingene as Babacan approached.

Taylor wasn't keen on leaving his friend. He was already starting to see him as he used to see Jafar in the early days, but they had no choice.

"That a good idea?" Jones asked as Taylor strode past him, tracing his steps towards the target on the console fixed to his arm.

"Probably not, but what are we supposed to say, we are here looking for an invaluable object that you could probably sell for an entire fleet of warships?"

Jones said nothing and followed on.

The ruined remnants of buildings were protruding from the dirt, but it looked as though they had been buried several storeys by the sand and dirt of the centuries.

"I guess the Krys worked out some kind of reversal of

terraforming?"

"We can do that now?" Taylor asked in surprise.

"Yes. It isn't perfect, but we can make habitable worlds. Could probably even go some way to fixing this place."

"I'm not sure the Aranui would even want it anymore. This place meant everything to them, the way it used to be. Sometimes memories are best left as they are."

As they past the shuttles, an Aranui Guardian stepped out and stopped before him. He held out the small steel ball from which Irala's likeness had been projected. The Guardian held out its left hand, and a hatch opened in the centre of its palm of a similar size.

"Guess this is how it works," Taylor said, placing the item into the Guardian's grasp. The hole sealed shut.

"How may I be of service?" the Guardian asked in Irala's voice.

"You have this mapping information, don't you?"

"Yes."

"Then lead the way."

The Guardian immediately took into full stride as they followed. He looked back one last time to check that half the troops had stayed to establish a holding base at the landing zone as he had requested.

"You are expecting trouble from them, aren't you?"

"Damn right, Jones. They aren't much developed beyond the Krys I used to know. If they see a single weakness, any opportunity which they can exploit, they will."

"That's rather sceptical," Alita said, rushing to join them.

"Yeah, well, you would be if you had seen half the shit I have. I trust those that have proven worthy of it. This lot looks like they'd slit our throats in the night, just to take the rations and weapons we are carrying."

"So you have just fed Babacan into the lions' den?" asked Jones.

"He can handle himself."

The Guardian led them to a domed structure that protruded a metre from the surface. It leant down, placed an explosive charge, and stepped back and watched. The charge ignited and was surprisingly quiet. Taylor stepped forward. A two-metre diameter oval hole had been cut as if with laser precision in to what was a half-metre thick ceiling.

"Got to get me some of those," he stated, leaping into the hole after the Guardian without question.

"Ah, hell," Jones muttered and jumped in after him.

He landed at the top of what appeared to be some sort of tower. It was fifteen metres wide and had a broad spiral staircase leading as far down as they could see. The Guardian and Taylor were already working their way further below the surface.

"Not a big fan of going underground when we only know one way in or out," Jones said to Alita.

"Why?"

"Getting buried alive? Think of a worse way to go?"

"I am sure there are plenty. Don't worry about it. We've got plenty of people to come looking for us if anything goes wrong."

"Providing the heat isn't too much. How do we know there aren't more of those Cingenes up there, or even down here? They could be waiting for their moment to pounce."

"Paranoid much?"

Jones did his best to smile. "Paranoia doesn't necessarily make me wrong. I don't like this at all. If it were this easy, then Irala would have come and done it himself a long time ago. There is something he isn't telling us."

"Probably, but Taylor will get to the bottom of it. He always does."

They went on for five minutes and reached the lowest point, the only lighting in the dark spaces the torches mounted to their shoulders and rifles. Taylor switched his rifle selector to flare and fired off three of the bright blue lights into the darkness beyond.

The light spread into every corner and revealed vast catacombs and arches, and yet there was nothing on the floor space at all.

"Guess they had time to clear out?" Jones asked.

The Guardian continued onwards without another word and led them through one room after another. It became deeper and deeper below the surface. The interior was much like the Aranui vessels, stark and simplistic, but with a level of elegance and sophistication in design not seen amongst the other races. They reached a room at the far end and what had been a huge and lavish fountain. It was built into the side of the walls and stood five metres tall, but there was no sign of any liquid. The Guardian strode right up to it and pushed its hand into one of the openings.

They heard a clunk and a mechanism activate. A square entrance two metres wide slid open. It had previously been entirely invisible to the eye.

"What is this?"

"The secret access tunnels of my people's government," replied the Guardian.

"And you know how to access them?"

"Only a handful of the most loyal subjects ever did. This was passed down to me many of your centuries ago."

They passed through three more such hidden doors before finding themselves at an elevator. It was barely large enough for ten, caked in dust, and yet several lights still flashed at a control terminal.

"No way, that can't still work," muttered Jones. He sounded worried.

"It will work for another three thousand of your years."

"All right, let's do this," said Taylor.

* * *

Babacan took a seat at a table that he had been ushered to. Benli and the rest of the Cingenes around him appeared unusually kind and friendly from the few experiences he had received from their kind in the past. Several large platters of food were delivered to the table that was now occupied in equal number by Babacan's people and Benli's. The leader gestured for Babacan to help himself to the food, and he could not refuse. He took what resembled flat bread. It was a bastardisation of what he was used to.

"We haven't seen any life beyond our own for many years," Benli opened the conversation, "Thought we had been left out here all alone."

"I had no idea any of our people had inhabited this world."

"No, you wouldn't. Only that wretch Jafar would know."

Babacan felt his spine tingle, as he sat up a little taller at the offence towards his master.

"That's why we are here, didn't you know?"

Babacan was starting to sense the trouble they were in, even if he didn't yet understand the situation.

"What did you do to warrant such a treatment?"

The Cingene leader looked even more aggrieved by his question than Babacan had been over the mention of Jafar.

"What did we do? What did we do!"

Babacan felt his hand reach for the rifle slung at his side. His hand stopped just millimetres from the grip. He knew he needed to avoid contact if at all possible. Benli leapt to his feet and began to circle the table. Everyone was on edge. The tension in the room was so thick, it was clear a fight was almost certainly imminent.

"Your Lord Jafar banished us to this world for doing nothing more than what our families have done for thousands of years. For as long as our people have lived."

Thieves, liars, and bandits; just because you have done it for so long, doesn't make it any better. You're still scum!

He thought it but held his tongue. Benli continued circling the table, and finally stopped beside Babacan.

"Your Lord Jafar, the saviour of our people. What did he do? Overthrow the greatest leader our people ever knew, and make allies of a pathetic and puny race of weaklings. Jafar is a disgrace to our people, and I would have him know it."

He smacked Babacan in the face as if to challenge him. The impact was enough to almost make him fall from his seat. Out of the corner of his eye, he saw the companion beside him squeeze the trigger on a pistol he had quickly drawn.

"No!" he yelled.

But it was too late. The shot rang out, and he felt blood splash into the side of his face. He turned just in time to see the body of Benli fall with a bullet almost dead centre between his eyes. Babacan was speechless. He saw a gun being raised and reached for his own. There was no choice.

CHAPTER NINE

They seemed to have been walking for almost an hour through a never-ending maze of rooms, corridors, and hidden doors. They saw not one sign of life, or even of anyone having disturbed the places they had been through.

"This is creepy," said Jones.

"You're only just now getting that vibe?" asked Alita.

The Guardian was approaching what looked like yet another dead-end that they expected to pass through, when it stopped.

"This is it."

"What?"

"The door I do not know how to open, Colonel."

"What? What do you mean?"

"I cannot open this door."

Taylor looked down in front of the Guardian. There

were two fine footprints in the dust. They were Aranui prints, long singe faded and barely visible.

"He did try," Taylor whispered, as he pointed to the evidence.

"Then why would he lie to us?"

"Because he cannot admit that he was here, Jones. He said it himself; it is a crazy story that not even his people believe. And now he cannot sneak away to try again."

"The Aranui live pretty much forever, and they are far smarter than we could ever hope to be. If he couldn't solve this, in what, hundreds of years, how are we supposed to?"

Taylor shook his head.

"I really have no idea, but I am not going to give up just yet," he replied calmly.

A light flashed, and an Aranui warrior projected before their very eyes.

"What is your purpose here?"

Most of them took a few cautious steps back, but Taylor stood his ground.

"I am Colonel Mitch Taylor, and I have come for the Tamir, the Pauri Tao."

"Why?"

"I was sent by one of your people, Irala."

"Why?"

"Because we need the spear. We need it once again."

"Not acceptable."

Taylor stopped to re-think his strategy.

"What does it want?" Alita asked.

"A genuine reason to give up the only thing it values."

He looked back to the Aranui projection that was awaiting his next attempt.

"You are Rua, aren't you? The great hero of the Aranui people?"

"I am the memory of Rua."

"What is it you really want from me?"

"To know if you are the one, one worthy of carrying the Pauri Tao. For if you are not, you shall never enter this chamber."

"Worthy?" Taylor asked.

"Yes."

He stopped and thought, trying to consider every possibility in his head. Almost fifteen minutes passed without a word from anyone as he tried to find the answer. He was starting to believe now that it could indeed be real, and that was only making him more desperate to lay his hands upon it.

"I fight with your people for our very survival. We fight against the same evil you did, Bolormaa and her spawn."

No response came.

Taylor collapsed down onto his knees in desperation, still trying to think of a way.

"Why have you come? You are not one of us."

Taylor was shocked to hear it. He had expected only responses to his words, and not a prompt.

Maybe there is more of Rua in there than just knowledge.

"Why me, and not one of your own? Your people will not believe in you and the Pauri Tao, but I believe, and I will do anything in the hope of one day placing my hand on such a weapon."

"Why? My people have no will to fight Bolormaa."

"But I do," pleaded Taylor, "I will fight her with my own hands until I draw my very last breath. I will fight her with everything I have, and all that I am. I will give my life to end hers, because I know what evil she is."

"Irala, he would not take up this weapon and fight?"

"No, none of your people will, but they can be led back to the right path. They are desperate. But I am not. Give me this weapon, and let me use it for what you showed the universe it could do."

"Do you have the convictions to fulfil this task?"

"I do. I would give everything for one chance at ending the curse that is Bolormaa. I do not ask anyone to do this task for me. I only ask that you give me the chance to do with my own hands what I cannot without the Pauri Tao."

Rua seemed to smile just a little, and then vanished.

"Where are you going?"

Taylor collapsed to his knees and screamed, "What more do you want from me?"

But they soon heard a vast winding mechanism begin to turn, and the enormous wall began to part, revealing it was four metres thick. A tear came to his eye when he realised they had done it.

"Unbelievable," said Jones.

The rest of the Immortals began cheering as the doors slowly drew apart. Alita rushed forward and wrapped her arms around his neck.

"Would you really give it all, everything you have?"

"Yes, he would," replied the Guardian, "That is why he was accepted. He gave what no other was willing to give."

"You knew Irala came here, didn't you?" Taylor asked.

"Yes, I know all that Irala does."

"And will he know this upon our return?"

"Yes."

Taylor knew he would take it hard, as it questioned his commitment, as well as that all of the Aranui, but that was trouble for another day. He got to his feet and strode through the doors. A series of lights came on. The room was little more than a very secure vault ten metres square. At the centre was a plinth and stand holding what looked like some kind of pole weapon.

"What is this?"

As he approached, he could see that it was not a weapon at all, but a staff with a bizarre hollowed dome atop it that was covered in inscriptions.

"Is that is?"

"No," replied the Guardian.

"Don't say that," Alita said, "This has to be it, or what are we doing here?"

Taylor reached forward, grabbed the staff, and lifted it from the plinth. It was lavishly decorated and inscribed in a language he did not understand.

"What's the deal?" he asked, thrusting it at the Guardian. It took the staff and carefully studied it. The others waited impatiently for some news.

"Well?" Jones asked after ten seconds had passed, and they had heard nothing.

"Is it the spear?"

"No, Colonel."

"No!"

"But there are clues here that may lead you to it."

"This really was a wild goose chase," Jones said.

"Well, that's just fucking great!" Taylor snapped.

He stood there speechless and about to ask another question of the Guardian when the primary comms console on his arm lit up. He accepted the transmission and shouted angrily, "What?"

He immediately heard gunfire in the background, and muzzle flashes lit up Babacan's face.

"We are under heavy fire. We need immediate assistance!"

Taylor saw it was an open channel to all parties in their task force.

Oh, shit! Does it get any better?

"Just hold tight. We are coming!"

"Bring that with us!" he shouted at the Guardian and

rushed back in the direction they had come from. As they ran, he hailed the Guam. Song quickly responded.

"Update me, Commander, what the fuck is going on?"

"Colonel, Babacan and his team are under attack. Our forces are attempting to reach them but are meeting heavy resistance trying to get into the village."

"They won't last long by themselves!"

"I know. What would you have me do? Every man, woman, and child in that little town is taking up arms."

"Do whatever you have to."

"Like what?"

Taylor stopped and took a deep breath, knowing he wasn't going to make it in time to make a difference himself.

"You can strategically strike from orbit with pinpoint accuracy, can you not?"

"Yes, we can, but at what target?"

Taylor took one last deep breath, realising what he was about to do.

"Target all grids with armed combatants, and neutralise."

Song could not respond for a few seconds.

"We'd have to wipe out the entire population to do that," she gasped.

Taylor nodded.

"I can't..."

"Yes, you can!" Taylor interrupted, "This mission and our people are more important than any collateral damage.

We did not cause this fight, but if we must do it, then so be it."

Song shook her head in disbelief.

"This is my mission, and you are under my command. Do it!"

"We'll never be forgiven for this."

"No," he replied solemnly, "And now you know the price we must pay to win this war. Do it, Commander, now!"

Song nodded grimly and relayed the orders.

"Aye, aye, over and out."

The transmission ended, and Taylor rushed back into a sprint to retrace their footsteps. They could feel the ground rumble around them as barrages rained down from orbit, and they knew they could not get there in time to do anything.

* * *

The sun was low in the sky when Taylor finally reached the surface and made his way towards the Cingene town. Far off they could already see smoke arising from several areas, and half the structures had been flattened. A fire still raged at the centre.

"Oh, no," said Alita in despair.

"What have we done?" Jones murmured softly.

The odd gunshot rang out in the distance as they

approached, but it wasn't the sound of war, but of execution and ending wounded lives. Several Human and Krys soldiers were being stretchered away to the Stormers, with more walking wounded behind them. Lieutenant Hartley stood on the outskirts. He was facing them, but seemed to look straight through them in a kind of daydream. His face was pale, and it was clear he was in shock.

Taylor strode up beside him and placed a hand on his shoulder.

"You okay, son?" he asked him.

"I will be," he finally replied with some confidence. Though Taylor couldn't tell if that was put on to save face. Taylor, who had first befriended the Krys, was accustomed to seeing their dead in great number, and it meant little to him unless they were friends. He had learnt to hate them so early on that no amount of their deaths bothered him. And yet he understood that it was a very different scenario for Hartley and the rest of them. They had grown up in a world where Humans and Krys were equals and lived together in peace. To him, it might as well have been Humans they had butchered.

"You did what had to be done, good work," said Taylor. He took his hand away and carried on to the rubble of the town. Bodies of fallen Cingenes lay scattered all around. There was none of their own amongst them. He hoped they had not lost any, but it was more likely they had been moved before he got there. A mound of rubble before him partially covered the bodies of two Cingenes. One that was clearly a youngster, and yet died with a gun in its hands which it was still clutching to.

He spotted Babacan at the centre of the village. Three bodies lay around him, and he stood frozen like Hartley had been.

"What the hell happened here?"

Babacan shook his head.

"There was nothing I could do. When the first shot had been fired, they would not stop."

"Well who fired first? Actually, no, don't tell me, it doesn't matter now."

Jones and Alita reached his side and were still looking around in absolute horror at the bodies all around them.

"Are there any survivors?" Alita asked quietly.

Babacan shook his head.

"You killed all of them?" asked Jones.

"We did what had to be done."

"You just massacred an entire town!" Jones screamed at him.

"That's enough!" Taylor barked.

Taylor needed to think for a minute. He knew this would weigh heavily on them all, and the only consolation would have been the discovery of the weapon they went in search of. This was going to knock morale, and he was trying to find some way to lessen the blow.

"Will this be a problem with your people, Babacan?"

"The Cingenes are not liked by many, but few would welcome the news of this."

"That's a yes, then."

Babacan nodded.

"These are nomadic people, right? Who is gonna come looking for them?"

Babacan shrugged.

"Then we bury the bodies and destroy what is left. Anyone who comes across this spot will assume they just moved on. In the grand scheme of things, no one is going to notice or care."

"That's it?" asked Jones, "Destroy the evidence and carry on?"

"It's our only play here."

"This isn't what I signed up for."

"Yeah, well, Alita, there's plenty in war that you didn't ever hope or wish for. It just is!"

"You disgust me," she spat and stormed off in anger.

Taylor couldn't blame her for it, but neither was there anything he could do to ease her suffering.

"This is wrong, and you know it," said Jones, "This isn't the old war you used to know. This will be discovered, and it will bring more trouble than you can imagine."

Taylor nodded.

"Yeah, maybe, but I fail to see what I can do about it now. We can't report this. Just as soon as we gained a strong Alliance, it could once again falter."

"And maybe it should. If we can't be honest about who and what we are, what was it all for? We're supposed to be the good guys!"

Taylor laughed. It seemed so inappropriate and unsettling to Jones that it sent a shiver down his spine. He waited for Taylor to calm down and fully explain himself, but it wasn't what he wanted to hear.

"My friend, in war there are no good and bad guys. There are winners and losers."

"That doesn't make it right."

"No it doesn't, but it isn't right or wrong. It is a tragedy, certainly, but we can neither change it nor make up for it. We can just go on doing what we know must be done."

"And what is that?"

"At its core, protect one another."

"Even when protecting each other means committing the most heinous of crimes?"

"If that is what is required to succeed, and survive, then yes."

Jones shook his head. He was starting to understand Taylor's logic, but it still made him sick to the stomach.

"You would do anything you had to, wouldn't you? You'd put a gun to our very own President's head and pull the trigger, if you thought it would improve our odds."

Taylor nodded. "I would, but I also have some limits."

"Yeah? Well we haven't seen them yet."

Taylor finally turned to look him in the eye.

"I would never sacrifice any one of you. I would do anything and everything to protect my brothers. You are my family, and so long as we remain strong, and we keep giving it our all, we have a chance."

"You talk as though we are the force that will tip the balance in this war."

"Aren't we?"

Jones was silenced as he thought back.

"I don't know who or what brought life into this world. All I can say is that somehow life has put me in this position. To lead, to fight, and to make a difference, but I can't do it alone."

Jones accepted it, but he still turned and left. He could not bear to stand amongst the bodies any longer. Taylor turned his attention to their alien friend.

"Babacan, dispose of the bodies and prepare the site to make it look right."

* * *

It was night by the time a hole had been dug by engineers' vehicles brought down from the Guam. The bodies were piled high, in what could only be grimly described as a mass grave, and the stench of the bodies only masked by the fuel they had been soaked in. Taylor stood at the head of the Human and Krys troops formed up to pay their respects. In one hand he held a burning torch, in the other, the staff they had taken from the Aranui chamber. He paced up and down the line looking from the bodies to the faces of his own troops. Finally, he came to a standstill.

"This was a tragic loss of life! We did not come here to start a fight, and nor did we! But do not blame yourselves for this. The blame rests entirely on my shoulders, for I should have perceived the threat for what it was and handled it differently. That is on me. But when you have lived through as many wars as I have, you will soon realise that these are the horrible realities of conflict. None of us will get through this without blood on our hands. The blood we chose to take, and the blood we had no choice to. We didn't find the weapon we came looking for, but we found this!"

He held up the staff and the torch to illuminate it.

"This is the clue we needed to keep going, and it is the first proof that we are heading in the right direction. I am sorry it had to go down this way, I really am. But we owe it to each other and to the Alliance to go on in our mission!"

He turned and threw the torch into the grave. The fumes instantly caught, and flames spread across the huge pit. Highly volatile, it went up like a flash of gunpowder and burnt through in just one minute, until there was nothing at the bottom of the pit but ash.

"Fill it in," he said to Babacan and carried on back to his Stormer.

The Guardian was the only one beside the craft. He passed the staff over to it. It seemed to study it intently, as Taylor sat back against the nose of the craft and watched the hole being filled.

"Tane Mahuta," said the Guardian.

Taylor's eyes lit up at the name.

"Your grandfather?"

"Yes, this was inscribed and signed by his very own hand."

Taylor leapt up in excitement.

"And you never knew of this?"

He forgot for a moment that he wasn't actually speaking to Irala, but it didn't matter, as the response would be the same.

"No. He always said that the Pauri Tao was in that chamber. He made me memorise the route."

Taylor looked at the magnitude of fine inscriptions on the staff.

"He couldn't risk it, tell you the full truth, but he has led a trail of breadcrumbs that you would understand. You can decipher this. He wouldn't have done it any other way. It is a map."

The Guardian looked at the inscriptions further and finally responded, "Yes, it is."

"Then you can lead us where it goes?"

"Yes."

Taylor felt some hope return. He had begun to doubt

the usefulness of the staff and the mission entirely.

"There may just be hope yet," he whispered to himself.

He looked back to see the machinery had already finished filling the hole.

"Everyone back to the boats! We have what we need!"

Few of them looked enthusiastic, but they were glad to be leaving the sight of such sorrow and regret. When they touched down in the docking bay of the Guam, no one was there to greet them. Taylor stepped out and held out his hand in front of the Guardian.

"Give it up," he ordered.

The Guardian opened its hand and the data sphere rose from its palm. He took it and left to head to the bridge with the Aranui staff in the other hand. No one followed him. Few knew what to do. He heard Jones order some equipment checks as he left. He entered the bridge and found a slightly lesser version of the despair and sadness he had just left. Song approached.

"Colonel, can I have a word?" she whispered.

Taylor shook his head.

"No, I'll have no secrets. Put me on with the fleet, with everyone."

She stepped back and did as he asked.

"This is Colonel Taylor. By now you all know what went on down on the surface. A lot of people died who didn't need to. We can't change that. But like this entire mission, you are sworn to secrecy. To utter a word of any part of this to anyone will be considered treachery, and will result in swift justice. I am sorry you all had to go through that, but it was not of our choosing. The important thing is that we are still on target and with minimal casualties. Stay strong. That'll be all."

He pointed to Song to end the transmission.

"The situation is what it is, no need to say another word. We have a mission to fulfil, okay?"

She nodded in acceptance as Taylor put the sphere down.

"Irala, you there?" he asked.

The likeness of the alien projected out from the object. Taylor held up the staff.

"Tell us what this means, and don't tell me you don't know."

"The wording is really quite clever. Only someone told the stories of my grandfather would understand what he meant."

"Yeah, it's a code, I get that, but what does it say?"

"It says to go to a world that my grandfather told many stories of, a mining world that was the site of two great battles. It is called Aratoro."

"And you know where it is?"

"Yes."

"Great, then get us moving."

"I can give you coordinates, but you cannot jump directly to this world. It is beside the Whatitiri Nebula. It is too difficult to navigate through a jump gateway."

"Show us," said Song.

Irala pointed to a map on the console beside the navigation officer, Osborne. They finally pinpointed the location and displayed it on a large projection for everyone to see clearly.

"There is no planet there," protested Nichols.

"Not that you know of," replied Irala.

"This is ridiculous. If there were a planet there, we would have it mapped on our star chats. This is just pure fantasy."

"If he says it's there, it's there."

Nichols sighed but did not say another word.

"That will take us a few days," replied Song.

"Good, then set a course."

He picked up the sphere and went to leave the bridge. Song followed him to the door and stopped him once again to whisper more privately.

"We can't have another experience like that. The crew are not able to withstand it. If this location does not yield any results, we should consider cutting our losses and returning home."

Taylor frowned as he shook his head.

"We don't give up because of some set back, Captain."

He looked over her shoulder. Nichols had been listening in. That was the sort of trouble Taylor didn't need.

"Just get us moving, and let's see where this takes us."

He went back to his quarters and stripped off his armour, collapsing onto the bed with a long drawn out sigh. He just lay there thinking about it all. It was the first time he had been able to let it hit him; he had to keep it together for the rest of them. At first the sight of the dead hadn't meant much to him at all, but as he realised the dreadful effect it had on the rest of his comrades, it was starting to set in. He felt paralysed by it all. Two hours passed and he could not sleep. Then there was someone at his door.

"Open!" he yelled.

Mitch let himself hope for a minute that it would be Alita. He quickly sat up in anticipation of her walking through the door, but he had no such luck. It was Jones. He slumped back down onto the bed with another sigh.

"How are you doing?" asked the Lieutenant.

"I've been better."

"Yeah, I know. I just don't know what to say."

"You must have something to say, or why did you come?"

Jones shrugged.

"Maybe because I thought you needed a friend."

Taylor grimaced, though it was actually true.

"It can't be easy...all the pressure that is put on you. You have this great reputation as the saviour of humanity, no small title. Not many believed it, but then you made them. You gave us all hope that the reputation you had truly was warranted, and you could earn such a title again in this time. You gave all that, and yet the reality isn't as clean and fairy tale as the history books would have you believe."

Taylor sat up, understanding Jones was at least seeing the big picture.

"It's going to get a whole lot worse before it gets better," he replied, "You imagine the worst things you have ever seen in your life, and then times that by ten, and have it happen every day for months if not years without end."

"But it's not all that bad, is it? I have read of your exploits. I know that in between all that chaos and death, you found plenty of good times."

"That's true, but you have to find them where you can."

"So fix it with her."

Taylor looked confused.

"Alita means something special to you. More than anything else in the life you now live. That is worth fighting for as much as this war."

Once again Taylor recognised some of Charlie in his ancestor, and that made him smile.

"I know," he said quietly.

"Still believe in this mythical spear?"

Taylor laughed a little. "One thing I learnt a long time ago was to hold on to hope, no matter how remote. I have to believe, or there would be no chance of finding it."

"You just don't strike me as a man willing to believe fairy tales, and the crew is starting to doubt it, too. The casualties we took down there are making them restless. Many wonder if you will just keep going until there is nobody left."

"We only lost a few, didn't we?"

"Yes, but it's hit them hard."

"That can't be the only reason they are restless?"

Jones shook his head.

"Well, come on, out with it," insisted Taylor.

"There are rumours. Some think you have gone crazy. Obsessed with some myth that is having you chase the rainbow."

"And what do you believe?"

"That you are too stubborn to quit, no matter what."

"Does that frighten you?"

He nodded. "A little."

"Well, it took a crazy man to get you this far. That's why I was taken out of the freezer. When all common sense and knowledge failed, you came to me. Maybe I am a little crazy, and maybe crazy is all that will see you through this."

Jones got up to leave, stopping at the door for one last word.

"It's not me you need to convince."

The door shut, and Taylor found himself settling into a deep and much welcome sleep. When he finally woke up, he had been out for nine hours, and appreciated just how much he'd needed it. He groaned as he got to his feet and headed out the door for the bridge. As he made his way down the corridors of the ship, he noticed a change in crew that he passed. They didn't look up to him as the superior and famed warrior that they had when he came aboard. Most acknowledged him, but they seemed wary of making eye contact.

Taylor was starting to understand what Jones was saying. It was a lot to ask for them to believe in the Pauri Tao. He had proven himself as a fighter and a leader, but he had no track record in this new endeavour. The crew had no reason to trust Irala like he did. The whole thing still sounded crazy to him, but he was willing to give it a chance. He stepped onto the bridge and received much the same response by all, apart from Song.

"We are fifteen hours from our destination, Colonel," she reported.

"Any sign of that planet yet? What was it called... Aratoro?"

"Nothing, Sir," replied Osborne.

"We're chasing thin air, might as well go home now before we lose anyone else," Nichols muttered.

"What was that?"

"You heard me, Colonel. This mission will lead to nothing but more death. You are obsessed with a fantasy."

Taylor strode up to Nichols.

"Whatever your personal feelings are, I suggest you keep them to yourself, Captain. This is not a committee run ship. If I wanted your opinion, I would ask for it."

"You don't give a damn, do you? We might as well be drones to you. You'd lead every single one of us to our deaths in the hope of more glory for your name."

Taylor smacked him across the jaw with a heavy backhand. The impact was both firm and surprising enough that Nichols was knocked over onto one of the consoles. Everyone froze in shock as he looked down with disdain and waited for the Captain to make some retort.

"Haven't got the balls, have you? No courage in your convictions?"

Nichols wiped a little blood from his mouth and slumped back down into his seat. Taylor looked around. The crew did not look favourably at his actions but were too scared to speak out against them. They were living in fear of him now, and that was a dangerous situation to be in.

"Don't think I would ever risk even one of you in any way for my own ambitions. I have none of my own. All I want is to win this war. Are people going to die in the process? Yes, they will. I will do my utmost to ensure I protect as many lives as possible, but you need to have a little faith in me, and each other. I can't give you any promises that we will find this weapon. That is not the way life is. Neither will I set a deadline as to when we might call off this search. For if I did that, we already accept defeat, and he who accepts defeat never wins anything. Stay strong and stay vigilant. You are the frontline, the first line of defence. A whole lot of people are relying on you."

Most seemed to take it quite well and stood a little taller for it, but Nichols would not even make eye contact with him. The Captain was sowing the seed of discord amongst them, and yet it was clear he had gone as far as he could to discipline the man. He turned to leave when Song interjected.

"Where are you going, Colonel?"

"To check on the wounded."

Nichols finally looked up, and it was clear he had not done so himself, despite his outburst. Taylor didn't need to say another word.

CHAPTER TEN

Taylor walked out of medical after having visited the wounded, when he stopped at the doorway. Alita was walking towards him and clearly hadn't expected to see him there. She stopped in her tracks. At first she looked a little awkward and angry, but that soon began to fade a little.

"I didn't expect to find you down here."

"Why, didn't think I cared?"

She shook her head as she began to cry a little.

"I'm sorry."

"For what?"

"You don't disgust me. It's just a lot to take in."

"I know. To me it was only a few years ago that I revelled in the sight of dead aliens. We didn't even see them as people at all. That came much later."

"You don't feel like that anymore, though?"

"Of course not. But it doesn't weigh so heavily on me. You build a tolerance in time. It's not a pleasant thing to grow tolerant of, but necessary in what we do. Otherwise you will become a quivering wreck and unable to go on living."

She staggered a few paces and sat back against the side of the corridor, collapsing down until her head was buried between her knees. She continued to cry. It was in this moment he was aware that he had asked too much of them. His new comrades were capable fighters, but they were not the veterans he used to know as the Immortals. His fearless companions had been through hell and could handle anything. He had expected the same of Alita and the rest of the new era of Immortals. They had it in them to be every bit as good, but only with time and experience.

"So that is the best advice you have? That over time our senses will just become dulled to the level that we don't care? What if I want to go on caring? What if it is what keeps us human?"

Taylor shrugged.

"I didn't say I had the perfect solution. But we work from the very core of what we need, survival, everything else is just a luxury."

He sat down beside her and placed his arm around her shoulders. She nestled in.

"I'll never forget what happened down there, and

we weren't even the ones who had to go through with it. You've won me over, but what about the rest of the crew?"

Taylor sighed. "They are restless..."

"They are more than that. There is talk of getting this ship turned around and heading on home."

"Mutiny?"

She shrugged at the thought of it, but did not respond. The situation was much more serious than he thought.

"You really think a crew would turn on me?"

"If pressed hard enough."

"Haven't I done enough to prove myself?"

"In many ways, yes, but what we are doing out here just seems madness. We have only a few ships. Were we to be ambushed, or attacked by any sizeable force, we would be utterly wiped out."

"Nothing ventured, nothing gained," he replied.

"And that would be fine if anyone on this ship believed in what we are searching for. A few weeks ago we had never heard of the Morohta. A few days ago we had never heard of this Pauri Tao. If such a valuable weapon existed, don't you think we would have known about it sooner? The myth at least, if not the location?"

Taylor had to agree with what she was saying.

"I understand, but I can't tell you why I choose to believe in this, beyond just the trust I have in Irala. Maybe his grandfather was making up grandiose stories, maybe he exaggerated, who knows? But somehow, deep down I know it exists. Whether we can find it or not doesn't matter. And however remote a chance there is, don't you think people want to be able to believe in something as fantastical as this spear? Is it not hope something beyond anything we can dream of?"

"Hope, is that what you think this gives us?"

"To those we left behind, yes. They know we were willing to give and put in everything we had for this. Don't you think that would inspire them to do the same?"

"But they don't even know about this mission or the spear?"

Taylor smiled as he shook his head.

"Wrong. I authorised the President to broadcast a pre-recorded message of mine forty-eight hours after we departed. Long enough for us to get free and not risk being pursued."

"But what if Bolormaa gets wind of it?"

"She's cut off, so we can hope she won't, and if she does, to hell with her! If she sends forces after us, then that only confirms the existence of the weapon."

"That is a very dangerous game to play. You are gambling with all our lives."

"Our lives were gambled the day the Morohta were discovered, the day you signed up for this job. The day you came into this war stricken universe."

"Doesn't mean we want to end them sooner than fate

intended."

"Fate?" he sighed.

"You keep saying you don't believe in it, and then at the same time seem to think you were put in this universe to serve some need, and certainly history would support that fact."

"Yeah, well, if you believe in all that crap, then I can't get you killed any sooner than the universe intended," he replied with a smile.

He got to his feet and offered out his hand. She gladly took it and was hauled up beside him.

"You sure know how to give a pep talk."

"I'm a people person, didn't you know that?"

She smiled as the last tear dropped down her face, but her expression soon turned businesslike.

"You need to make this right with the crew before it is too late."

"I get that," he replied, stroking her face.

Nichols' voice came over the comms.

"Colonel Taylor, report to the bridge, please."

"I guess they are singing my song." He kissed her forehead and made to leave.

"I'll stand by you, no matter what, you know that right?" she said as he walked off.

He didn't need to say another word, but it meant a lot. Now he just had to win over the rest of the crew. As he got halfway to the bridge, he found Jones.

"Think we have made it to the planet?"

Taylor looked down at his console and shook his head.

"It's too early. We can't be there yet."

"Maybe something else of interest has come up?"

"Yeah, maybe," he replied with little enthusiasm.

He was trying to think how to smooth things over with the crew, but he couldn't find a way. He had said all he had to say and given them all the hope he possibly had to give. He stepped onto the bridge. Nichols was at the centre. Beside him were two security guards either side of Captain Song who looked sullenly at the floor.

"What is this?"

Nichols stood tall and proud for the first time in a while and responded with a commanding and strong voice.

"Colonel, you have continued to put this crew at unnecessary levels of risk and have broken the laws and the very moral foundations of the Alliance! You have disregarded the concerns of your crew, and continued to lead us on a path to destruction. I no longer consider you fit for duty."

"And what does the Commander have to say about this?" Taylor spat.

"Commander Song has failed to work in the best interests of this ship and her crew. I have relieved Song of her command and assumed full control over this mission."

"How dare you! You have no such right, you pathetic little worm!"

He reached for his pistol, but he felt Jones' hand grab his other arm. He looked to the Lieutenant who gestured for him to look to their side and rear. Six of the crew had carbines trained on them.

"What the hell are you doing?" he asked Nichols, slowly letting go of the grip of his pistol.

One of the guards stepped forward and ripped it from his holster, as well as his Assegai from his other flank. He only just resisted the urge to turn and strike the man down, knowing he could not afford to start a battle on the bridge.

They'll never come back to my side if I draw first blood.

"The President authorised this mission, Captain. He will not looked lightly upon this," stated Jones.

"President Isaacs will understand why we had to do this when he sees what happened on Moana. You can't go through this life getting away with every crime, Taylor. You're a savage creature that should never have been set loose in this world."

"And you would not be alive if he had not," replied Jones.

"That does not excuse the things he has done. Escort Commander Song, Colonel Taylor, and Lieutenant Jones to the brig."

Taylor could see the Captain honestly believed he was doing the right thing. He didn't particularly like the man, but he could see in his eyes this was not being done because of his own ambition, but for the fear of the loss of life for him and his crew.

"Just tell me you are going to get to that planet and give it a shot? It's less than a day to reach it, what is one more day?"

"One more day of risk. I cannot put this crew through it. They have suffered enough. We are returning to Ares, and you will face the charges in a military tribunal."

"As will you," he snarled.

"Captain, I'm tracking something on a collision course," said Osborne in a panicked tone.

"What is it?"

But before any response came they felt the ship rock, as an explosion rang out. They all stumbled a few paces. Taylor saw the guard behind him stagger. It was the opening he needed to grab the man's weapon, and yet he looked to Jones who still shook his head.

"This isn't the time," whispered Jones.

"What the hell was that?" Nichols asked.

"I am not picking up any vessels in the area."

Nichols rushed to Osborne's console. Everyone saw the panic in his eyes. Another explosion rang out.

"We're in a minefield. Look where you have brought us!" he yelled to Taylor.

"Get them out of here!"

"Wait!" Taylor shouted, "Ask yourself, Captain, if there is a minefield here, why? Is it not likely here to protect something of value? Like a planet that you believe does not exist because your maps say it doesn't?"

"Put this on screen!" Nichols ordered.

A large projection map displayed hundreds of mines for as far as they could see.

"Tell me how we get through this!"

"We're already a good way through. The guns should be able to handle plenty, and this old girl can take the rest," replied Taylor.

"You just live on hopes and dreams, Colonel. You gamble lives away without any consideration at all."

"Activate defence grids and turn us about!" Nichols ordered.

They could see tracer lights as the railguns opened up on several of the mines, but a few seconds later they heard a massive blast, and the ship was rocked. The lighting fluctuated from the impact, and half the screens on the bridge failed.

"We have lost power to the engines!" one of the crew shouted frantically.

"Start auxiliary engines."

"They are out, too, Captain."

Nichols froze for a minute, realising they were floating through the minefield with no power at all.

"Use docking thrusters to bring us to a stop!" Song ordered.

"Get her off the bridge!" Nichols insisted.

"Wait," Jones interrupted, "That is no mine."

They all fell silent and looked to where he was pointing. A narrow torpedo like object was soaring towards them.

"I thought you said there were no vessels sighted?" Nichols stammered.

Jones had seen this before when he had first encountered the Morohta; the boarding Stalkers that almost ended him before the war had started.

"That hasn't come from a ship. We're about to be boarded."

"Target that incoming object and destroy it!" Nichols gave the order.

The weapon systems opened up and obliterated the target. But soon after another four appeared on the scanners. Their weapon systems destroyed another, but the next hit the hull and disappeared from the scanners. The guns continued to fire at the rest as Nichols barked his orders.

"Secure the bridge. Send out marine parties to defend our borders!"

"Let us help," Taylor pleaded.

Nichols shook his head. "You will remain under arrest. Take these officers to the brig!"

"Come on, Captain, for whatever your differences, you have two of the best combat officers at your disposal. Use them," Song pleaded.

"Don't be a fool," added Taylor, "Don't get us all killed

because of some dispute between us. We can settle our differences after we survive this. Think of the crew first. You need us."

But Nichols said nothing and turned back to the screens. Four security personnel led them off the bridge.

The blast doors shut behind them, but Jones knew that would not be enough to protect them.

"Keep your eyes open," he said to the guards, "These Stalkers are the nightmare from hell you wished you never had to encounter."

"Just keep moving."

Jones grimaced, feeling naked without any weapons, though at least they still wore their suits.

"What's the play here?" he whispered to Taylor.

Taylor shrugged.

"If they don't want our help, there isn't a lot we can do."

"Nonsense, I've never seen you give up over any hurdle before."

"You can't help those who refuse to be helped. Nichols has to learn from his own mistakes before he will come to me for help."

"Those mistakes will probably cost him his life."

"Then so be it."

Jones was surprised to hear how lost Taylor sounded. He had not seen him like it before.

"Will you not fight this?"

Taylor shook his head.

"Why? I help Nichols survive this, and he will only have me behind bars and before a tribunal. You know he can. What happened down on Moana was wrong, and every court in the Alliance would be forced to act upon that. If I don't have the support of those around me, I don't have anything at all."

"Yes, you do," Song joined in, "The crew is scared. Of course they are. But Nichols is the one feeding their fears. The crew will support you, given the chance."

They heard gunfire ahead, and the guards around them looked terrified.

"Not ever been in a gunfight, have you?" Jones asked them.

It brought a small smile to Taylor's face. Jones was quickly becoming the veteran his namesake had been.

"Just keep your wits about you, and be ready for anything," added Taylor.

The gunfire became a little louder, and they heard sharp cracks as the alien weaponry fired its high-energy weapons. A few flashes lit up ahead. They were getting close to the action.

"Think those carbines can touch a Stalker?" Song asked.

"I know they can't," replied Jones.

"Sergeant, you are leading us all to our deaths," she said to the man leading them.

"I have my orders."

"Don't be a fool. You'll get us all killed."

He ignored Taylor. "Come on, move."

They had two of the guards at their front as they went forward into the affray.

"Can't say this is how I ever wanted to go into a fight," whispered Jones.

"Our only hope is our Assegai. You get a chance, you take it."

Gunfire rang out ahead, and the bodies of two crewmembers flew into view as a Stalker took the bend and tossed them aside. It was a six-legged variant with a single weapon mounted to its torso. It was a little bulkier and cumbersome than the ones Jones had first encountered. Its steel armour looked like an ancient relic.

"Fire!" yelled the Sergeant.

The two at the front took aim and opened up with uncontrolled sustained fire. It didn't matter. The shots glanced off the armour of the spider like Stalker as it rushed towards them. Shots hit the two men in front. Taylor and Jones held them up as Human shields as they drew out their Assegai from the belts of the fallen soldiers. They went forward to meet the metallic creature in close combat. Shots hit the bodies in front of them, and one glanced off Taylor's armour before they came head to head with the creature. It drove one of its legs through the body Taylor was carrying. It passed through with little resistance, stopping as it brushed his torso armour.

He threw the body aside with the creature's leg still impaling it, causing the Stalker to tip to one side. He used the small opening he had to drive his Assegai into its leg at one of the joints. The tip penetrated right through and severed the limb. Blood flowed out all over the corridor.

The Stalker quickly responded by lashing out with one of its other legs. Taylor narrowly avoided the strike, but it slashed into Jones' left arm just above the elbow. He screamed in pain and was thrown back a little, but it was another opening for Taylor. He kicked out another of the creature's legs, and it tumbled into the wall with its flat underbelly presented to them. With one quick leap, Taylor was on top of the creature and drove his Assegai deep until he felt it impact and burn into the bulkhead. The creature was pinned to the wall. He drew out the blade, and it slumped down. He looked back. The two other guards stood shocked and stunned by everything they had seen.

"If you'd listened to us, your two buddies here would still be alive. Willing to follow my lead now?" he snapped.

They were both shaking in fear, and that helped them to agree quickly, anything to not have to face the enemy alone. Taylor picked up one of the carbines from the dead guards and thrust it into Song's arms.

"Time to get your hands dirty, Sir."

She accepted the weapon but didn't look too impressed.

"I thought this couldn't hurt them?"

"It can't, but you can at least piss them off," he replied.

Taylor activated his shield and led them on.

"What do you think their intentions are?" Song asked quietly as they cautiously retraced their steps and towards the gunfire ahead.

"I'd say they are part of the minefield. They can't know who or what we are."

"So destroy us? That's all?"

Taylor nodded. It wasn't much relief.

"This minefield must have been here for a hell of a long time," she added, "Since the Morohta left..."

"Not likely. We've never found any sign of their existence until Kepler. This field is probably Krys."

"So the Stalkers could be a new addition?"

"Maybe."

"Then the Morohta might well know we are coming."

"That's just a risk we are going to have to take," replied Taylor.

"This mission just gets better by the minute," joked Jones.

They could hear a hive of activity ahead and stopped to wait in ambush for whatever was going to take the bend. It sounded like multiple targets coming their way. Jones noted the two crewmen were pale and terrified. They were on the very edge. He looked back just in time to see a glimmer of movement as someone turned into their corridor. One of the crew fired a burst, and the other joined in even before they realised what they were looking at. Shots bounced from a Reitech shield, and a hail of abuse came their way as they leapt back into cover.

"Hold your fire!" a voice boomed.

Jones knocked down the barrels of both the crew beside him as he shook his head.

"You could have just fragged one of your own," snapped Taylor.

Babacan stepped out and looked far from impressed that he had been shot at. He looked surprised to see the Commander with Taylor, but he did not question it. Four of the Immortals were with him.

"What's our situation?" Taylor asked.

"I thought you might know," replied Babacan.

Taylor shook his head.

"It's complicated, what do you know?"

"We were boarded by at least four Stalkers. We have taken one down and found the body of another."

"One for us, too," replied Jones.

"So we aren't in the clear yet. We're heading for the bridge. Keep sweeping the ship," Taylor ordered.

Babacan rushed onwards with his team.

"Don't we need them?" asked one of the crewmembers. He was looking a little sheepish having fired on one of their own.

"We can handle this. You just keep your eyes peeled. Follow up and watch our asses, okay?"

They nodded in agreement and Taylor went on.

* * *

"How long until we get engines back?" Nichols asked. He was frantic.

The young female officer he had appointed as his XO looked terrified and unable to answer.

"Lieutenant Capek, how long?" he insisted.

"I...I don't know, Sir. Head of engineering is doing everything he can, but we have sustained severe damage."

"I need answers, not problems."

Capek didn't know what to say, so she said nothing. Another explosion rocked the ship as a mine struck the hull.

"Can you bring this ship to a stop or not?" demanded Nichols.

"I think so. If we can..."

"Just do it!" Nichols yelled. He almost sounded hysterical.

He looked around for someone else to offer him something, but all he saw was warning lights flashing from hull breaches. All camera feeds but the one outside the entrance to the bridge was now lost. As Nichols watched this single remaining feed, he saw a Stalker step into view and casually stroll up to the door. Its single body-mounted weapon opened fire on the two guards outside, and they were cut down before they could even fire a shot. Several of the bridge staff gasped in horror.

"Don't worry, it won't get through those doors. Nothing can!"

But his voice was full of doubt, and yet he still hoped. The Stalker stopped a few metres in front of the door.

"Get our marines up here!"

"Sorry, Sir, but our internal comms are down."

"Is nothing on this damn ship still working?" Nichols screamed.

The entire bridge crew sat frozen and staring at the screen as they fixated on the creature. It seemed to study the blast door for just a moment, and then it fired eight shots around the opening. It lunged forward and threw its bodyweight at the door. It came crashing down inside the bridge. The Stalker just stood on the fallen door triumphantly as if studying them all and waiting for someone to make a move. It appeared to be eyeing up its prey.

"What do we do?" Capek asked.

"Nothing we can. It's over," replied Nichols in a defeatist tone.

The Stalker made two steps towards the Captain when it suddenly twitched and righted as if it had been prodded with something. It staggered forward just a few paces, slumping dead in front of Nichols with an Assegai buried deep into its torso. As it fell, it revealed the source of the impact. Taylor stood at the far end of the corridor leading to the bridge. Jones and Song were with him. They jumped into action and strode onto the bridge as the triumphant defenders that they were.

Nichols was frozen in terror. He made no attempt to reach for a weapon.

"Captain Nichols, update me. What is our condition?" Song asked firmly.

Nichols was so surprised by the question he seemed unable to speak a word.

"Answer the Commander," Taylor ordered.

"We...we are dead in the water..."

"Then let's see what we can do," replied Song.

"I...I...don't...am I under arrest?"

Taylor shook his head, but Song answered him.

"Negative. You made a mistake, Captain, and we have all made them in our time. What lesson you should take from this is that we are stronger together. You will resume your position as XO of this ship, and do so in a manner that seeks to serve and protect all who serve aboard her. This mission is about more than just one person, one ship, or one race. Whether you question its relevance is not at all a reason to question the authority that the Colonel and I hold. Just remember that the next time you consider munity, it is because of Colonel Taylor that you are still alive today."

Taylor wanted nothing more than to strike Nichols

down and send him on his way. Fortunately for Nichols, he could see that the crew morale was low, and Song's leniency was the right way to go.

"I...I am sorry," said Nichols with his shoulders slumped low, and his eyes looking to the floor in front of Taylor's feet.

"Don't be sorry. Do your job."

Taylor had to muster everything inside him to be polite to the Captain, but somehow he managed it, and it did not go unappreciated by the crew. Song still saw it fit to ram the message home.

"Like it not, this ship and this crew needs Colonel Taylor, and the Alliance needs this ship. Enough dissent, from now on we go forward together!"

It was clear to Taylor that Song was still considered as much an outsider to them as he was, and yet she was doing a damn good job of becoming something far closer to all their hearts. Song took a deep breath and resumed to her duties.

"Have the Massri and Curlew come alongside us and engage towing braces. They can guide us out of this mess while we get our engines back online."

Nichols looked shocked that he hadn't thought of that, and it was some relief that he was once again in the right place. He smiled as he went about his business, clearly glad to relinquish the responsibility of the ship to Song.

"Not easy is it, having responsibility for everyone

around you?"

Nichols turned to see Taylor standing beside him and asking the question.

"No, Sir."

"We can't always make the right decisions. Sometimes we just have to make do with the best we can manage, or the one that will save the most lives. When you learn to appreciate that, you will earn your own command."

"Thank you."

"For what?"

"For not destroying me over this. I was a fool. I panicked and made the wrong call."

"Yes, you did, and you won't be the first one to do something brash for all the right reasons, and then realise your mistake afterwards. We all do it, but we also learn from it."

Nichols nodded slowly as if in thought and then went back to his duties.

Song approached Taylor. She looked relieved as she took up position by his side.

"As much as I hate to say it, that attack couldn't have come at a better time," she whispered.

"Yep, nothing like the risk of death to shake things up."

"So what I asked about before, these Stalkers. Do you think they have been waiting here for what, hundreds of years? Or are they are the result of this modern conflict?"

Taylor shrugged.

"I wouldn't begin to speculate without some evidence. We are alive, and they are dealt with. That's all that matters right now."

"And if we pass through this nebula and find a Morohta fleet waiting for us the other side?"

"Then we'll turn tail and run as quickly as we can."

Song shook her head. "I don't like this at all. If we were going to pass so far into uncharted space with potential enemy presence, we should have come in far greater number. A dozen warships would have barely made me feel safe."

"That wasn't my choice to make. You can take it up with the President."

"I don't have his ear like you do, Colonel, nor would I want to."

He wouldn't have wanted it either. He'd do anything to stay away from the politics and management of the war, if he knew he could rely on those in position to do the job right. He stared out into space and the nebula that reduced their view range to only what the Human eye could see. Explosions lit up the foreground as the gun systems continued to blast a path through the minefield. It was a waiting game now, and Taylor could not help but feel excited to see what was on the other side, no matter how terrifying it might be.

* * *

Taylor was lounging on his bed when he found himself drawn to the videos Dubois had left him. They had hit hard before, and he wasn't ready for them, but he needed something from his old life to hang on to. Some reminder of what he was still fighting for. He played the next video in sequence and smiled as she appeared before him overlooking a city from a great height.

"Taylor, look, repaired and as good as new. The Eiffel Tower. You remember fighting for this city and this magnificent landmark," she said, walking along one of the walkways high up the structure and looking down at the beautiful parks and rivers beneath.

"This is what we all fought for, and finally we have it. I pray someday you wake up so that you may see for yourself what we achieved. I still think of you all. Those we lost, and those who still remain. Come back to us, Taylor."

The door light went. He paused the video and yelled, "Come!"

Jones stepped through and opened his mouth to speak when he spotted the woman frozen on the screen.

"Who is that?" he asked, and it was clear he at least partly recognised her.

"Coco."

Jones instantly realised who she was.

"Please, continue."

Taylor shook his head and ended the video.

"No, some things are too personal to share, at least for

now."

Jones did not argue the point. He saw it meant a lot to Taylor.

"What can I do for you?"

"Have you considered what a high profile target we will become if we get our hands on that spear? Every power hungry fool will want it, and that doesn't even begin to include the Morohta. You know that much power corrupts?"

"All too well."

"Then what are we to do about it?"

Taylor laughed.

"Let's worry about finding the thing first. You worry like a gambler planning how to spend his millions of winnings."

"You don't seem to worry at all. Someone has to."

"We all have our part to play," he smiled.

"Anyway, what I really came here for. Engines are up and running, and we are now fully operational."

"Good to know. We may just make it through all this yet, then."

"Have you ever doubted it?"

Taylor smiled in response, and that was all Jones needed to know.

CHAPTER ELEVEN

"Three minutes, Commander," said Nichols.

Taylor stood on the bridge in full armour with his Morohta hammer attached to his back. He was ready for anything. With all the concerns that had been levied at him now, he half expected to find a Morohta fleet ready to blast them into dust. However, nobody said a word as they counted down the seconds to breaking out into open space.

Taylor thought of what the world might look like.

Come on, be there, you son of a bitch. Aratoro, are you just a dream?

The clouds of the nebula seemed to part before them as the bow of the ship broke out into the vast open space beyond.

"Weapon systems at the ready!" ordered Song, "If we

find any substantial resistance out there, I am jumping us out, anywhere," she whispered to Taylor.

"Think you will be able to do that?"

"Yes, we couldn't jump here because we had no idea of the geography of the area, and the ever changing environmental effects may make it impossible to ever do so. But find us some open space here, and we can go run where we want."

"Let's hope that isn't necessary."

After what seemed an age, they pierced the last clouds of the nebula and broke out into open space. Many of the crew gasped at what came into view. It was not the shock they had all feared, but a beauty they could not have dreamed of.

"I don't believe it," stated Nichols.

That brought a smile to Taylor's face. What lay before them was an arid world with the remains of a vast space station still floating in orbit. The structure was identifiable as of Aranui construction, but had long since been abandoned. Taylor lifted the sphere and activated it so that Irala once again stood before him.

"Is this it? Is this Aratoro?"

"Yes."

"Just as he said it would be," added Song in amazement, "Scan the area!"

"I've got faint energy signals coming from the surface. That's all," replied Capek.

"No sign of a fleet or any ships at all?"

"Negative," replied Osborne.

"Hell, yes, we might just pull this off yet," muttered Taylor.

"What are your orders, Colonel?"

"Take us is."

"Set a course, launch fighters."

It took them almost an hour to close the distance and have a good view of the former station.

"Do you believe now?" Taylor asked Nichols.

"I always wanted to, Sir, but yes, I can see there is hope now."

Taylor retreated to Song's side so that he could talk to her privately.

"If anyone has any inclination that we are here, and the reason we have come, we will have a whole world of trouble coming down on our heads. So you be ready for anything and anyone, you hear?"

Song nodded.

"And no matter what, you protect the Aranui ship. It is our ticket out of here."

When they finally reached the planet, they had aerial shots of what looked like the remnants of a vast city. Though it seemed almost entirely industrial. It stretched forty kilometres long and almost as wide.

"This must have been one hell of a mining operation," said Taylor.

"Yes, but before my day," replied Irala.

There appeared to be no signs of life in sight, or any explanation as to what was mined there.

"Looks like a wasteland to me."

"It was not always this way, great oceans, canyons of precious metals, and pockets of gas. Every nutrient and resource you could ever think of."

"What happened?" Song asked.

"War."

"Someone must have hit this place hard and destroyed the ecological system," added Jones.

"Will we even be able to breathe down there?"

Irala had no answers, but Nichols was carefully studying the data before him.

"For a few hours at a time, any more and the toxicity and dense molecules will start to clog your windpipe. Much longer and you will suffocate."

"Mmm, could be worse."

"Underground you will be safe, with clean air," added Irala.

"How can you know that?"

"He is right, Lieutenant. I don't know what it is, but something under the surface is working to keep the air clean," said Nichols.

"There are still living inhabitants here?"

"No, but the world was intended to be self sustaining. Anything not damaged beyond use will still be operational."

"You people sure know how to build things to last."

"We must, for your lifetimes are merely a fragment of ours."

"Any more advice before we do this?"

Irala shook his head. Taylor put the sphere in his webbing, and the projection powered down.

"I'm taking my people plus another twenty of the marines with me. I'll take Lieutenant Hartley. He's proven himself."

"Will that be enough?"

"If it isn't, then everything else you have wouldn't make a difference."

"Then I wish you luck, Colonel. I have every faith in you and your ability to find this great weapon, if it indeed does exist."

"Stay sharp, Commander, and be waiting for us if we come running."

Ten minutes later he stood before the team and three Stormers. He held the Aranui staff from Moana in one hand, his hammer on his back, and rifle in the other hand. The Aranui Guardian stood next to the unit with its hand outstretched for the sphere, which he provided.

"How many of you believe in this spear, the Pauri Tao?"

None answered, though he wasn't sure if that was because he had sounded rhetorical, or just that they were sceptical.

"How many of you believe in miracles?"

Still nothing.

"Well, I do. Do you know why? Because I have witnessed enough to know they can happen. But they don't happen by chance or some great mystery. They do because of hard work, perseverance, and a cast iron will to succeed. That is what I need of you today. Suspend disbelief and believe in something that seems beyond reason. I remember the day I first saw alien life. Seeing it with my own eyes was the only thing that would convince me I wasn't being strung along as part of some great prank. Well, I ask that you rise above that. The only evidence we are going to have is finding what we are looking for. I need you to do what I could not all those years ago. Believe and have faith in this. For if there is even the remotest of chances of this weapon existing, it could yet change the course of the war which we will face soon enough."

"We're with you all the way, Colonel."

Taylor nodded to Jones and then gave the order, "Load up and move out!"

They climbed aboard the Stormers to begin yet another mission. Taylor looked around to see all the Immortals were fast becoming vastly experienced combat veterans. Increasingly, he knew he could depend on them now, but they needed a great success or victory to cement their confidence, and their reputation.

"Do you believe half the things you say? Or do you just say what you know people need to hear?" whispered

Jones, sitting beside him.

Taylor thought about it for a moment and then shrugged. He really didn't know the answer himself, but it didn't seem to matter either way. He looked up to his team and spoke openly.

"If you get your hands on this spear, you trust no one with it, you hear? It does not leave this group, not unless every one of us has fallen. You do not trust the President with it, nor Irala, nobody."

"The Alliance won't like that at all."

"Yeah, well, tough shit. They don't even believe in this weapon, so it's none of their business."

"But Irala?" Jones asked.

"Let's not forget that everyone in this world has their own agenda. I've been gone so long I don't know whom I can trust and with what anymore. What I do know is that those here with me now, I can trust. You have proven that many times over. So when you get this weapon, you protect it with your life, right?"

The interior of the ship lit up from viewscreens displaying the skies around them as they entered the dusty desert like world.

"Is it still as exciting? Visiting a new planet the first time?"

"To tell you the truth, Jones, excitement has never been the emotion I would use to describe it. Every single new world I have ever stepped foot on has led to death, destruction, and regret."

"Wow, that's a happy thought."

"Take me back to Earth any day, so long as some lunatic isn't lurking out there waiting for their chance to make us extinct."

"Is that what you still want, after all this time?"

"Of course, isn't it what any man would ever want? Look around at all this, is this what you want?"

"I wanted to explore and discover new and exciting things."

"And how is that working out for you? Guess you got a little more than you bargained for?"

Jones could not deny it. "Maybe it's worth the price."

Taylor turned his attention to the viewscreens. They had a lower viewpoint of the old industrial city now. There was no sign of any power or life. Dust and sand had overtaken many of the structures and all of the streets.

"You can't tell me this isn't exciting, no matter how much danger is involved?"

Taylor smiled and looked over to Alita. She was genuinely as excited as Jones was. For a moment he was reminded of how that felt, and began to get a little sense of it himself. Hunting for an ancient and powerful weapon was certainly a fascinating prospect, and yet doubts over its existence barred him from getting too enthusiastic.

He looked down at his console; they were very close to the landing zone now. He was about to mention it, when Alita slowed the craft and brought them in for a landing on what looked like the floor of a large hexagonal shaped building. The walls were long gone, and the hard standing only just visible through parts of the sand. As their engines blasted the surface, the sands were parted, and the steel like base of the old building became clear. It was adorned with Aranui symbols. They had no idea what it meant and had little reason to ask.

The landing gear touched down, and Taylor was the first at the door as usual. The ramp lowered, and the acrid air that he had been expecting struck him. It wasn't pleasant, but it was still preferable to having his face sealed and contained within his suit.

"Hard to imagine what this place would have been like if Irala's account is accurate," said Jones.

"We're heading one klick north. Hartley, have a squad cover our left flank, the other the right. Rest of us are going down the middle!"

"Do we even know what we are looking for?" Jones asked, as they stepped off the foundation of the building and into a broad road.

"Well?" Taylor asked the Guardian.

"The staff is the key. He who can read the staff can find its lock."

"Riddles? That's all we need."

"That staff was left for Irala to find, and for him to understand. We have to rely on him working out its directions."

"I still don't understand why he couldn't come with us. If this mission was safe enough for us, why not him?" asked Alita.

"Because Irala is irreplaceable."

"Right, I see how it is."

"Yep, that's what we're paid for."

They passed from one building to another. Many were still mostly intact, others looked like they had been heavily bombed during some long ago conflict. There appeared to no sign of life anywhere they look, but just as they thought they were going to have an easy run of it, an explosion blasted out on their left flank. It shook the ground beneath them.

Taylor was on his feet in seconds and rushing across to where he knew one of Hartley's squads was. He came to a quick stop on finding the body of one of the marines in the Lieutenant's arms. Both his legs had been blown off, as well as his left forearm. The Lieutenant had a piece of shrapnel buried in his right arm, a deep cut on his left, and dust and cuts on his face.

"What did this?" Jones asked despairingly, as he caught up with Taylor. He took a knee and looked cautiously around the area, his rifle at the ready. Taylor could see the crater where the explosion had originated. It had launched the fallen marine several metres through the air, and a deep crater remained from the blast.

"Land mine."

"What? Surely not?"

"Yes," replied Hartley solemnly.

"From who?"

"This is Krys technology, and likely left over from the last war," said Babacan.

"We were so preoccupied with this spear and the Morohta that we forgot all the other dangers that exist in this world," added Jones.

The medic appeared at Harley's side, but he would not let go of the fallen marine for a while.

"Ground scanners on, let's not have another accident like this!" Taylor shouted to everyone.

He activated the device on his console that would scan the surface in a five-metre radius around his person. He bitterly regretted his mistake in not having done this when they landed.

It's my fault. I should have thought of it.

Hartley was soon patched up. He looked sad for the loss, but he didn't take it out on anyone but himself.

"Let's get on with this mission, Sir," he said quietly.

Taylor nodded in gratitude for his resolve and gestured for them all to continue. He headed back to the main road where they had come from. Within two minutes the scanner on his arm began to bleep, signalling it had detected something. He raised his fist and brought them all to a halt. He drew out a mine clearer grenade from his webbing and rolled it across the floor in front of him. He slowly took a few paces back. The grenade ignited, with its signature deep pulse sending vibrations through any buried devices to ignite them. A second later the mine blew, just as the last had. A few shards of metal and rocks hit Taylor's shield, and dirt and dust settled over the top of him.

"Any more surprises we can expect to find?" he asked the Guardian.

"I do not know."

"Did you not fight in the last war?"

"Yes."

"And did you fight on this world?"

"For a time, yes."

Taylor shook his head. He realised he wasn't getting anywhere. He got up and pointed for them to go onwards. Another scanner began to bleep soon after, and it was Jones' turn this time in a repeat of the clearing he did. Another three explosions rang out on their flanks as they made their way to the destination, when finally the three groups found themselves descending on one crossroads. Taylor's console confirmed that it was their destination. He was looking around in every direction for something, anything. But all he could see was more dust and rubble.

"There's nothing here," said Alita.

Taylor drew out the Aranui staff and paced around the perimeter of the crossroads.

"Any ideas?" he asked the Guardian, but there was no response.

He walked towards the centre of the crossroads, though it looked as bare and dusty as the rest of the road.

"There's nothing here, Colonel, what do we do?" Jones asked.

Taylor could see the exact marker on his console lay at the centre of the roads, and so he approached it cautiously with the staff held out as if it were hazardous material.

"What are we doing here, Colonel? There is nothing here! It is a waste of time," Hartley shouted.

It was apparent that the loss of his marine weighed heavily on him. Taylor knew he had to find some answers soon, or the mission would fail. He reached the centre of the crossroads and looked down. There was nothing but sand at his feet. He simply stood there, hoping for some miracle, as he was all out of ideas. Finally, he lowered the staff, and the base touched the sand. As it made contact, a light sparked as if the base had contacted metal and some electricity passed between the two.

"What the hell was that?" Jones shouted.

Taylor remained still and waited. For ten seconds nothing at all happened, and then a bright blue light appeared between his feet. It began to trace a line forward and then drew a two-metre circle in the sand around him. He looked up at Alita.

"Is this really it? she asked.

The ground began to rumble, and then a wide section in front of Taylor began to lower into the ground. The troops around him scattered as more layers in front of that dropped further down. A dust cloud was thrown up as they waited to see what was there. Then the dust began to settle, and a huge stairway beneath the surface was revealed to them. Taylor looked up at them all marvelling at the sight. It was giving them all hope.

"Could it be? Could it all be for real?" Alita asked again.

But no one had an answer. Taylor took the first step, and the others followed without another word. The stairway was cut from rock and appeared entirely natural, aside from the fact they knew it could not be; as it was created by some kind of mechanical mechanism they could not yet see. They kept descending until they were almost a hundred metres down, and the ground began to level out.

"Wow," Alita said, as the space opened up into a vast and high chasm. Orbs emitting light were fitted every five metres down either side of the chasm. Two narrow paths clung to each side, and the space between them looked like a dried up waterbed.

"Must have been some kind of underground lake," said Jones.

"What do we do now?"

"Looks like there is only one way to go, Alita," replied Taylor, and he went forward.

His team followed him while Hartley took the right

side, though they appeared to be following the same route.

"Could this place really have remained secret all this time?"

"Not exactly the kind of place you would come looking, is it? An abandoned mining planet, and nothing left here but sand and wreckage," Jones answered her.

Taylor looked around. They were all starting to believe now. There was some hope, and he just prayed that it would be paid off in full. They got half a kilometre along the chasm when both paths joined and stopped before a tall steel door. Besides the lights, it was the first thing that was not created by nature since they had entered.

"You don't build a door like that unless you want to protect something valuable," stated Jones.

It was covered in a thick layer of dust and had clearly not been opened in living memory, at least a Human's memory.

"This mean anything to you?" Taylor asked the Guardian.

"I have never seen or heard of this before."

Taylor stepped up before the door, and as he got within arm's reach, a light flashed and a soldier was projected before them. He was wearing full armour from head to toe, and a cloak, as if in ancient ceremonial armour. It had the shape and size of the typical Aranui. It seemed to study them for a few moments before noticing the Guardian, but it said nothing. He then saw Babacan and still said nothing. Taylor glanced at the Guardian and then his people, but they all looked to him to make the first move. He lowered his rifle and addressed to the warrior.

"My name is Colonel Mitch Taylor, of Earth. I represent the Alliance of Human, Krys, Cholan, and Aranui peoples. I come here in search of the Pauri Tao."

Almost a minute passed before they received a response.

"The Krys are our enemy, and I do not know Human nor Cholan. But here you stand, a race I do not know, with both Aranui and Krys by your side? What trickery is this?"

"No trick. We are allied in a common cause to fight the Morohta, and their leader, Bolormaa."

The warrior was gazing across at his troops but snapped back to Taylor upon hearing those two words.

"The Morohta have returned?"

"Yes, and that is why we have come. We need the Pauri Tao. You know of its power. We will need it in this fight."

The warrior was silent and seemed to consider the information he had given. Taylor knew he had little else to offer and could not afford to risk offense by making a story up.

* * *

Song watched in horror as she saw the explosion ring out on their overview. She could see the fallen marine in close detail and his horrific wounds.

"I don't envy those who have gone down there," said Nichols.

"No, and something tells me this will not be our last casualty before we are free of this place."

They observed the entire events on the surface unfold and marvelled as the entrance to the underground vault was revealed, and everyone followed Taylor beneath the surface. Song didn't like this at all, not being able to see what was going on. A minute had past, and she was already getting anxious. She wanted to contact Taylor, but she knew she must let him work.

"Sir, I am getting some readings off the starboard side, ten klicks out," said Osborne.

"What? What kind of readings?" she snapped.

"Looks like a sort of engine signature, but it is so faint."

Song felt her heart drop, but she did not panic.

"Activate weapon systems! Launch all remaining fighters, and deploy marines at all sectors!"

The crew hesitated for just a second, as they could not see what she was getting at.

"Do it now!" she screamed.

Nichols quickly relayed the orders, but he still could not understand the Commander's concern.

"What is it?" he whispered to her.

"We are not alone here. The Morohta have come looking for their weapon."

"How can you know?"

But Song avoided the question.

"Osborne, bring us up a screen tracking that energy signature!"

"There is nothing there, Commander. I have already checked visuals."

"Just do it!"

The screen seemed to track through empty space. Suddenly, they noticed a glimmer as sunlight reflected off something and flared before them. For just a split second they glimpsed a ship that was less than half their size. It soared through space with utter grace as it made its way to the planet's atmosphere.

"Target that reading, lead by twenty metres, fire when ready!"

The gun batteries of the Guam opened up with a salvo. The first few shots found no target, but as they continued to trace the signature, a dozen impacts ignited on a ship. Its invisible shielding failed and so revealed itself. Another salvo caused several explosions on the surface of the hull before finally the ship came about. Several smaller craft dropped from it as it made its way right for them.

"Send word to Taylor. We are under attack by Morohta forces!" Song ordered.

But before the order could be acted upon, a hail of gunfire smashed into the Guam and battered here already weak structure.

"We have lost all communication, Commander," replied

Osborne.

Another wave of gunfire smashed into them and rocked them where they stood.

"What do we do?"

"Only thing we can do, Captain Nichols, stand and fight. Give them everything we've got!"

* * *

Taylor still waited silently. He half expected to come under attack in any moment, and was already kicking himself for bringing Babacan along. It had never occurred to him that it would be a problem until now. At last the warrior responded with stern and succinct questions.

"Who sent you?"

"Irala."

"And who sent him?"

"His grandfather, Tane Mahuta," replied Taylor confidently.

The alien seemed a little alarmed and briefly hesitated, but then responded in a deep voice that carried through the chasm.

"I am Tane Mahuta."

The warrior's helmet retracted to reveal an old and scarred Aranui elder. The Guardian quickly approached and held out its hand where Irala was projected. They looked at one another for a few minutes, as if communicating without speech.

"You trust this Colonel Mitch Taylor?" the warrior finally asked.

"Yes."

"You trust him with your life? And with the great responsibility that the bearer of the Pauri Tao must endure?"

"I do."

"Then enter, and claim it. May it serve you well."

The hologram vanished, but no one said a word. The huge door parted at its centre and began to retract back into the walls.

"Could this really be it? Have we really done this?" Jones asked.

"Incoming!" a voice cried.

It was followed by automatic gunfire. Behind them several of their team engaged a dozen Stalkers who were skittering across the chasm floor, walls, and ceiling at high speed. Two were immediately knocked out, but more quickly filled the chasm, in what seemed a never-ending wave of the enemy.

"Can this door be shut again?" Taylor asked the Guardian.

"Yes," it responded and pointed to the control panel on the other side.

"Come on, in through here!" Taylor shouted.

They quickly retreated through the doorway while

continually laying down covering fire. Taylor waited at the doorway with the Guardian until the last had made it through.

"This door will not hold them for long. I will buy you time," said the Guardian.

It held out its hand and released the sphere into Taylor's care. It then stepped out from the shelter of the doorway and opened fire with its arm-mounted cannons. Several impacts brushed off its armour, and Taylor took a few more shots at one of the nearby Stalkers before turning to the control panel. He hit the switch as the Guardian had shown him. As the door began to close, he looked back for just a moment. A glimmer of movement in the distance sent a tingle down his spine.

It was the unmistakeable shape of a Morohta Prince. He wanted to believe it wasn't true, and in the shadows he wasn't sure, but he had no time to stick around to find out. He rushed on after his team. They found themselves at yet another junction with three passageways splitting off in different directions.

"Can never just be easy, can it?" he sighed, "Same as before, go!"

He looked back. As the door slowly continued to close, Stalkers were pouring through the gap. He could still hear the Guardian raining down fire on their attackers, but certainly it could not do enough to stop them. He took a few shots and rushed onwards into the middle passageway.

"All teams, Stalkers are hot on our tail. Keep moving and watch your asses!" he yelled through the comms.

But he soon realised no signal was getting through, and once again they were in a communication blackout, as he had known all too often.

"This spear better exist now, Colonel, or we're done for!"

"That's far truer that you want to know, Jones!"

"What do you mean?"

"You remember Ganbaatar? I think he's right behind us."

"You're joking?"

"Think I would joke about that?"

"We're finished," he said hopelessly.

"Not yet," replied Taylor, as he continued to run.

CHAPTER TWELVE

"Commander! The Massri has fallen!" Nichols screamed. He sounded terrified.

Song looked to the viewscreen at her left side. The ship had almost been cut in half. Fire raged in more breaches of the hull than they could count, and lifeboats were jettisoning in every direction. She looked to her other flank, and the Curlew was being pounded as heavily as they were. She could see they simply weren't doing enough damage quickly enough.

"Have the Aranui vessel and our fighters jump out twenty klicks, and instruct them to return three minutes later."

"What? What are you doing?"

"Just do it, Captain!"

Nichols knew well enough from experience not to

doubt Song any longer. He sent out the order and watched as they fled. A volley of fire smashed into their hull. They couldn't withstand much more. The Morohta vessel was a fraction of their size and stood alone, and yet its armour was thick and weapons powerful.

"Prepare to launch an EMP."

"To what target?" Nichols asked. He was confused.

"Right between us and that ship."

"We'll be completely defenceless," pleaded Capek.

"We should have jumped out with the others. We can't win this," added Osborne.

"Enough!" Nichols hollered, "Have faith in your Commander, and follow through with her orders!"

They were shocked to hear it, but Nichols' confidence in her made them doubt no longer.

"EMP launching in five, four, three..."

They were rocked once again by heavy gunfire from the Morohta ship.

"Two, one, launch."

They watched the device soar out before them.

"Open blast shielding."

The shields across the windows of the bridge slid open, and they could see the EMP soaring towards the Morohta vessel before it ignited. All systems died, and they were left in the dark. Only the natural light of the sun stopped them from being in complete darkness. They watched with joy as the Morohta ship floated as lifelessly through space as they did.

"Their systems will almost certainly recover quicker than ours."

Song smiled at Nichols as she counted down the time in her head. A light flashed beside them, and the Aranui ship and their fighters appeared. Their weapon systems instantly started laying into the stricken Morohta vessel, to the cheers of the bridge crew around the Commander.

"Good call," whispered Nichols, leaning in beside her. She slumped down in her chair in relief. She was shaking.

"Thank you for keeping your faith in me," she replied.

"What about Taylor?"

"There is nothing more we can do for the Colonel right now. Whatever is down there, he is just going to have to handle it himself."

* * *

"You got a plan beyond that of running?" Jones asked. He was almost breathless.

"Keep going until we find the Pauri Tao."

"That's your plan?"

"Unless you have got a better one. I don't know any other way out of this, and unless you want to turn and fight a Prince of the Morohta with what you have, I suggest you keep running!"

Gunfire rang out behind them. The Stalkers were

closing in quicker than they could cover the ground. As Jones and Alita continued to lead the way, Taylor stopped and allowed the others to pass until he reached the tail end of their squad. Babacan, Antos, and Bailey took up positions beside him and waited for the Stalkers to come. Each of them held out their shields with their rifles just peeking around the defensive energy.

The first Stalker rushed out, and all of them opened up on full auto. It was tossed into a sidewall under the weight of fire and pinned by it. They killed the Stalker outright, and it slumped to the rocky ground. The next came at them and received the same treatment. Taylor drew out a grenade and primed it.

"Sir, charges down here could wall us in!" Bailey shouted.

"Let's worry about staying alive first. We'll worry about getting out if we accomplish that," replied Taylor with a smile. He tossed the grenade down the corridor and ducked back as it blew.

"All right, let's go!"

They rushed onwards. Jones and the rest were waiting for them a little further ahead.

"Why did you stop?"

"You think we know where we are going?" Jones asked and pointed to a series of further forks ahead.

Taylor raised the sphere, and Irala appeared once more.

"Shed some light on this please," said Taylor.

Irala's likeness studied all that was around him and looked up to the symbols over each of the caverns.

"That one," he said confidently and pointed to the far right.

"You are sure, Colonel?"

"It's good enough, Jones," replied Taylor, and he ran on down it.

He came out at a vast opening as large as they had discovered when they first came underground. All was quiet for a moment, but then it was broken by the echo of automatic gunfire from Reitech rifles off to their right side. In the distance one of Hartley's squad rushed out from an opening and firing wildly. One threw a grenade back from where they had come. Even as the explosion rang out, several of the Stalkers came into view. One had two legs blown off but was still clawing its way towards them. Another two rushed out from the smoke of the blast.

Taylor and his team took aim from their slightly elevated position and lay down fire in support until the last of the creatures were put down. He hurried to their side but found two of their number was missing. One had lost his left arm, severed close to the shoulder, and two others were bleeding from leg wounds. He knew there was nothing they could do but keep moving. The squad's sergeant was badly beaten up, too. His left ear was missing, and his jaw burnt where a shot had come close to taking his head off.

"Stay put and protect this position, you hear, Sergeant?" Taylor ordered.

"Aye, aye, Sir," the Sergeant replied confidently and pushed a new magazine into his rifle.

Taylor ran across the opening in the vast chasm.

"Think it's wise to leave them there?" Jones asked.

"It's the best we can do with them. They can't keep up with us, and we could do with the support."

"You're just leaving them to die?"

"No, Alita, I'm leaving them there to fight. This mission may yet be the end of us, but I am not going to give up yet. We need every opportunity we can to find this damn thing."

"You are still holding out hope of finding the Pauri Tao?" Alita shook her head.

"Damn right, we need a miracle, and that's it."

None of them could think of anything better, and Taylor wasn't giving them much time to dwell on it. They carried on and passed down a long chasm that was narrower than the rest. The walls were deep and exquisitely carved, but they did not have time to stop and inspect them.

"How big is this place?" Alita asked.

"What was it even used for?" asked Jones.

"Questions that don't need to be answered at this stage," replied Taylor.

They heard gunfire at their backs where the squad they

had left were engaging the enemy. Taylor and the others stopped for just a moment, wondering if they should go and help, but they knew they could not.

"It can't be far now. Let's keep moving!"

But soon they could hear the skittering sounds of a Stalker at their backs. Taylor thrust the sphere into Alita's hands.

"Keep moving!"

The squad rushed on past him, and he waited patiently. The creature stormed into view on the ceiling where he least expected it. He raised his rifle and fired a burst. He hit it several times, but it wasn't enough. It leapt from the roof. Two more shots penetrated its body, but it landed on top of him, and he was smashed down onto his back. He could just about bring his rifle to bear and fired another burst, finally managing to throw the creature off him. He got to his feet. Its stinking blood now dripped from his armour, and it made him gag.

"Disgusting," he muttered and quickly left to join the others. He reached the group. They had stopped completely. He pushed his way to the front of them. They were standing in front of a narrow stone bridge. It stretched a hundred metres across a canyon that was so deep they could not see the bottom, only the darkness that filled it. The bridge had no barriers at all, and any who slipped from it would surely fall to their deaths.

"Let me guess, that's where we need to go?"

"Yes," replied Irala whose projection now stood beside him.

"Colonel! We've got a problem!" Watkins called.

Taylor rushed to his position. He was looking through an opening to their flank where dozens of Stalkers could be seen weaving their way through cover and heading their way.

"Never can catch a break, can we?"

Jones pushed in beside him to take a look at the problem.

"Take a few with you and keep going. The rest of us will hold them here."

"Sure? Or you just don't want to cross that bridge?"

Jones smiled.

"Maybe, but you also need some time to work this out and not be running like crazy fools. Go, do what we came all this way for."

Taylor didn't wait another second.

"Babacan, Hariz, Antos, with me. Rest of you dig in, you're with Jones!"

He rushed to the bridge that was more of a frightening causeway. It appeared to have no supports or suspension at all. He wondered if it could even sustain their weight, and yet he had no choice but to try.

"You know I don't like heights?"

"You're a pilot, Alita," joked Taylor.

"Yeah, but where I sit is in a comfy seat with wings and a few thousand horsepower to keep me going forward."

Taylor laughed, but he also completely understood what she meant. It was a daunting obstacle, but they waited for him to lead the way. He took a deep breath and stepped onto the first stage and was amazed to feel it held firm.

"See? Not to bad," he grinned.

Although it was clear to them all that he didn't believe it. Gunfire rang out from Jones and several of the others starting to engage the enemy. He turned and continued on at a steady pace in order to maintain his balance, and to get across as quickly as possible.

Keep going! Keep going, just a little longer, he told himself.

He reached the other side and breathed a sigh of relief, offering out his hand to Alita who was following behind. She saw no shame in taking his hand at the last stage and was hauled onto the platform on the far side. Out of the corner of his eye he saw a flash and hauled her forward. She was thrown onto her front, and a pulse of energy flashed past him where she had just been standing. They both landed hard, and Taylor looked up from the ground. He saw Irala's sphere rolling along the floor towards the edge of the chasm. He reached forward for it, but could not stretch far enough. It toppled over the edge and vanished into the chasm.

Fuck, but I'm not going to sew doubt amongst my friends. I'll just have to manage without it.

Taylor was quickly on his feet. Babacan and Antos were already returning fire, and off to their side they could just make out another larger causeway running almost in parallel. A single Stalker fired at them, but well aimed shots pierced its armour, and it fell into the darkness of the chasm.

"There must be another way in," said Antos.

"No shit," replied Taylor, thinking what that could mean, "We'll sort that problem out when we get to it. Come on, we have to keep going!"

They passed through a large archway, and it opened out into the first and only structure they had seen since the security door that resembled Aranui technology. It was a vast hall with steel columns supporting the centre. It appeared completely empty, but there was an opening on the far side, and one to their left. The left entrance must have been where the Stalker was trying to make its way to. Taylor pointed to the far side entrance.

"That's got to be it!"

They continued at a quick pace and kept a keen eye on the side exit and everything around them.

* * *

"We've got power back online!" Nichols said excitedly.

The viewscreens fired up around them, and Song glared at the Morohta vessel burning beside them. It was still intact but disabled and severely damaged.

"Shall we board her? Who know what we might find."

Song shook her head at Nichols.

"No chance. The Morohta are not a people to be toyed with, Captain. We have won this battle. Let us not risk another soul. Target all weapon systems on that ship, and tear her apart."

Nichols relayed the orders, and they watched as every gun on the starboard side opened up and smashed into the stricken vessel. The third salvo finally punched right through the hull, and the crewmembers were sucked out into space. Some looked humanoid in shape, unlike others they had seen before. Song looked around at the crew, and many looked away in shame and despair.

"Don't you dare show any sympathy or remorse here!" she yelled, "If you learn anything from this mission, and from the Colonel, it is that there is no space for weakness in this war. The Morohta are like nothing any of us have ever experienced, an evil so awful that they are the things of nightmares. Celebrate this victory, and take pleasure in their demise."

They watched the Morohta ship tear apart for a few moments.

"What about our troops on the ground, Commander?" asked Capek.

Song shook her head.

"There is nothing more we can do for them right now. We need all hands on deck, and all marines on duty. The threat may not be over yet. Deploy shuttles to bring in any lifeboats you can recover from the Massri. It's time to lick our wounds."

Nichols was staring down at the planet now.

"So there is nothing more we can do for the Colonel?"

It was surprising to all to hear such concern coming from the Captain for the man he had grown to hate so vehemently, and yet it was clearly sincere.

"The Colonel can handle himself. If anyone can pull this off, it is him. Bring up a view of the landing zone."

The feed showed the three Stormers intact and alone. They could see no sign of the Morohta craft that had headed for the surface.

"How long do we give the Colonel?"

"As long as he needs, or as long as we can safely maintain this position."

* * *

A single Stalker appeared at the side entrance as they passed it. They all opened fire on the move and killed it before it was able get more than two shots off. One was absorbed by Alita's shield and the other passed overhead. They reached the entrance at the far side. It was a large chamber, and in the centre the remains of an Aranui warrior in full ceremonial attire. It looked just as the hologram of Tane Mahuta had.

"Think that's him?" asked Alita.

"Would make sense."

They looked around the bare room, but the only decoration was a depiction of an Aranui warrior. It appeared as if carved from marble and was set in stone from the floor. At the base it just said 'Rua'. Taylor remembered that name. The great warrior Irala had told him about.

"This must be some kind of shrine."

"It looks like it, but how does that help us?"

"If that is Irala's grandfather, then he must have been here for a reason, a guardian until the very end. We need to look around."

"For what?"

"Anything, Antos, any opening, doorway, just anything."

A pulse hit the entrance, and the burst sent hot energy over them. One of the fragments burnt into Antos' ear. He cried out in pain but spun around and opened fire on the Stalker that was approaching. Taylor rushed to his side to assist as the other two continued to look for any clues. They gunned down the creature and another that was behind it, when they lowered their rifles in horror at the creature which entered the hall where the others creatures had fallen.

"Oh, shit," said Taylor.

"I can't find anything," said Alita.

She stopped as she saw the two of them looking out of the archway in fear and awe. It was then that she spotted it and felt her heart sink.

"No, it can't be."

Taylor looked back at her with sadness and dread.

"We cannot beat that, and neither can you. But we can buy you some time. Keep looking. It has to be there. Antos, on me."

Taylor released the rifle strap from his armour and dropped the weapon to the floor. He knew it would be no use in this fight. He drew out the Morohta hammer from his back, and Antos drew his Assegai.

"Just stay alive as long as you can," whispered Taylor.

The Morohta Prince pranced through the hall arrogantly, appearing to have absolutely no concern at all. Taylor and Antos stepped out from the hallway and up to meet the creature halfway. Both sides stopped to eye one another up. Taylor held himself with supreme confidence, but it was all just an act. He knew how devastatingly powerful the Princes could be.

"Ganbaatar, I can't say I am glad to see you survived our last encounter."

"Ganbaatar? How do you know that name?" asked the creature.

"Guess you aren't him, then. Last time I clapped eyes on him he was falling to his death on Khar Els. That was before we blew it to hell."

The Prince looked confused and angry all at once.

"You lie."

Taylor shook his head and smiled.

"Guess you haven't been home in a while. I am Mitch Taylor from Earth, and I am here to end you, your brothers, and that bitch you call a mother."

He could see his attempts to rile up the Prince were working.

"I am Sarnai, Prince of Morohta, and I will be the last thing you see in this life, pathetic little Earthling."

The Prince threw its arm forward and a chain lashed out. Taylor got his shield up just in time, but the chain wrapped over his arm. He was pulled and launched through the air in the direction of the Prince, who cut at him with a single edged blade that pitched forward towards its tip. It clearly had massive cutting power. As he passed the Prince, he just managed to place the shaft of his hammer between them, and the cut was brushed off. But he hit the ground hard as the chain unravelled, and he rolled rather ungracefully to a stop, smashing into one of the support columns.

"This ain't gonna be fun," he gasped and quickly got back to his feet.

Antos rushed in to his aid. To Taylor's surprise the hulking marine managed to duck under the chain after seeing it being used against him. He thrust in for one of the Prince's legs, but it was retracted, and the blade of his falchion like sword came crashing down, aimed at his head. Antos lifted his shield at the last moment, which took the blow, but the force pushed him down onto one knee.

"I just can't see anything!" Alita screamed in a panic.

She looked behind her for just a moment to see Antos kicked across the room and Taylor leap in for a second attempt. She forced herself to look back. She was running her hands up and down the lengths of each wall, desperately trying to find any sign of a doorway or opening, and Babacan was frantically doing the same.

"There is nothing," Babacan said despairingly.

"Don't stop! There must be something. There has to be. If there isn't, then we're all dead." She went back at it in a state of frenzy.

Taylor ran forward and swung with his hammer at the creature's lead leg. He swung it about his head as he leapt in again for a second strike. The Prince was surprised by his speed and aggression, and the hammer struck his left shoulder. The power of the blow caused his shoulder to drop slightly, but he quickly recovered and cut with all his power. The blade slashed through the steel grip of the hammer and cut deeply into Taylor's armour at his stomach. He felt the blade just cut a few millimetres into his skin. Another cut came at him, and he brushed it off and spun out from yet another as he drew his Assegai.

Antos let out a war cry, in part to psych himself up, and partly to take some attention from Taylor. He rushed in and jumped up onto waist of the creature and tried to thrust for its guts. He was stopped dead. The Prince took hold of his arm and punched him at his core. The impact was so powerful that he was thrown through the open archway and across the room Alita was searching. He then crashed into the likeness of Rua.

Alita turned and watched in sheer terror to see him drop unconscious to the floor. She had no idea if he was still alive, but her attention turned to the stone depiction of Rua. It had shifted slightly from its place, and part of it had come out from the wall. She paced up to it and ran her hands along the edge. She could just see a small green light emanating from a small gap that had been created.

"That's it," she whispered.

Babacan had seen it happen and discreetly joined her.

"Come on, help me," she said quietly, hoping not to attract the Prince's attention.

They hauled Antos out of the way without even checking if he were alive. They knew it didn't matter if they could not succeed in their mission. She went back to the stonework and held a grip before applying all her strength.

Taylor noticed what they were doing and smiled. He faced Sarnai with a grin on his face.

"You really believe in the myth of the Tamir?" Sarnai sneered.

He began to laugh.

"Clearly you do, or you wouldn't be here."

The Prince's face changed to a serious expression, and

he knew he had hit a nerve. He rushed at Taylor with a series of uncontrolled attacks from his legs and sword. Taylor kept moving back, taking parry after parry until finally the chain was launched at his legs. He jumped over as it passed him and went forward with a quick lunge, thrusting in at one of the creature's legs. The Assegai cut a little into the metal like skin but was brushed off. Sarnai grimaced. He had at last succeeded in hurting him, but not badly enough. The Prince smashed Taylor's shield down and swung the heavy chain into his face. He was knocked back, and blood spewed out from his face and nose. But Sarnai did not let up.

"Come on, Babacan!" Alita urged him.

They both grabbed as firm a grip as possible and gave it everything they could muster. After several attempts, they felt it give way and prise open. It revealed a small room lit by green beam lighting. At the centre was a small plinth. She stepped up to it expecting to see the weapon, but she had no such luck. There were only the mounts for it and an empty display.

"No, no way, it can't be," she said and fell to the floor exhausted.

Babacan appeared at her side.

"Look," he said. His hand traced a cut out on the top of the plinth and between the mounts. She could see what he meant immediately. It was the exact shape of the head of the Aranui staff they had found on Moana. She rushed to the archway. Taylor and Sarnia were facing off against one another. Taylor was bleeding from a wound in his shoulder where he had been cut deeply, as well as to the face.

"The staff!" she cried.

He knew exactly what she meant, even if he didn't know why she needed it. The urgency in her voice meant everything. He drew out the staff from his back and threw it towards her, but Sarnai saw what they were doing. He launched his chain to catch the staff as it flew through the air. Taylor threw his Assegai, and at the last moment it struck the chain and set it off course. The chain was wrenched from the Prince's grip as the Assegai tore it away from him. The staff landed in Alita's hands, and she threw her own Assegai back across the room for Taylor.

"What's the matter, scared of what we might find? That thing that doesn't exist, the mythical weapon that can slay your kind?" Taylor asked.

Sarnai went forward in a rage now and swung with five heavy cuts against Taylor. He avoided all but the last. He pushed his shield up, but the force beat it down, and the blade buried into his collar and cut another deep wound. He let out a cry of pain but struggled back to his feet. Sarnai did not stop. He kicked at Taylor's legs, and he crashed to the ground.

The Morohta then turned to Alita and rushed at her, but Taylor painfully forced himself back up and picked up the chain. With all the strength he had left, he threw it at Sarnai's legs. It wrapped securely around them and stopped the creature in its tracks.

Alita pulled the head from the staff and placed it in the cut-out. It was a perfect fit, and light glowed from its core. They could hear mechanical mechanisms begin to turn. They looked back into the centre of the room. The Aranui's body moved across as two hidden doors in centre of the floor opened. They watched in amazement as a gleaming golden asymmetrical blade arose before them. It was adorned with shining purple inscriptions so that the blade appeared to be moulded from fine crystals. A white steel shaft a metre long bore the blade and was similarly decorated with gleaming black Aranui inscriptions.

"It's real," Alita whispered, and tears rolled down her cheeks.

Taylor felt his neck almost snap as he was struck with the backhand of Sarnai. He had barely turned back when he felt his sword cut deeply into his chest. He raised his arm in defence, but it was no good. Sarnai cut down. The blade cleaved into his vambrace, which was all that stopped his arm from being severed. He felt the last of his energy reserves fade as Sarnai grasped his throat, lifted his feet off the ground, and plunged the tip of his sword into Taylor's torso. The thrust was so powerful that the blade exited through the backplate of his armour.

"No!" cried Alita as she turned to see the sword plunge

through Taylor's body.

Sarnai stared at her as he drew the blade out of Taylor and tossed him aside.

"Come on, you son of a bitch," she whispered to herself.

He let out a shrill cry and rushed to the archway. Babacan charged forward to meet him, but with one heavy swing, he was smashed aside. The Prince, who was larger than the archway entrance, crashed through the architecture and leapt at Alita. His sword was held up for a crushing blow. As he descended towards her, she dropped down onto one knee and raised up the Pauri Tao. She wedged the butt into the side of her foot and pointed it right for the centre of the Prince's chest. His face turned to fear, but he had no time to redirect.

The blade pierced his body and thrust through and out of his back. It stopped at two barbed horns on the shaft, and he came to a lifeless stop before he would crush her. Black blood that resembled oil poured out from the wound and from his mouth as he struggled to breath. She pushed with all her strength, toppled him over onto his back, and pulled out the spear. The alien Prince tried to speak but could only gasp. Alita held the spear up high. She drove it through his back and slashed to the side until it severed his head.

She dropped down to one knee and gasped in relief, marvelling at the beautiful blood drenched weapon in her hands.

Taylor, she thought and rushed to his aid.

She charged out through the archway. There were more than ten Stalkers beside Taylor's body. She stopped and raised the spear to show them their Prince's blood dripping from the blade, and then lifted his head with her other hand. They looked for just a few seconds before running in terror.

* * *

Commander Song stood at attention with half of her crew at the docking bay as they watched the three Stormers come in to land. They still didn't know what to expect. Dozens of marines waited there amongst them with their rifles at the ready.

"Think they really found it?" asked Nichols.

"Something went on down there. We must pray they did," replied Song.

The door to the first Stormer opened, and Jones and Babacan staggered out carrying Taylor across their shoulders. All were battered and wounded, but Taylor was not able to support his own weight, and he looked barely alive. A medical team rushed to their aid, and he was soon placed on a stretcher.

But the crew still waited in anticipation of the news. Alita stepped out next with several others of the Immortals.

They appeared as if they had been fighting for weeks of brutal combat, and yet most were still standing on their own two feet. Everyone came to a standstill. Alita stepped up to the centre, and all eyes were on her.

"We went down there in search of a weapon that few of us ever truly believed in. Taylor believed, and he was willing to, and almost did, give everything to find it!"

As she spoke, Taylor fought off the medics giving him aid and tried to pull himself to his feet. He reached for Jones to support him, and with Babacan's help he slowly made his way over to Alita, and she carried on.

"The Pauri Tao is real, and here is the proof!" she shouted. As she did so, she tossed the head of Sarnai into the centre of the room. It rolled to a halt as blood splattered across the deck in a gratuitous display.

She turned to Taylor as he reached her.

"Do you want to do the honours?"

He shook his head. She pulled out the weapon from behind her back and thrust it into the air for all to see. Few could believe it for a moment, and there was an eerie quietness, until Nichols began to clap. Everyone else in the room soon joined in. Song was shaking her head in disbelief and began to cry with happiness at their success. Taylor finally raised one hand to have a word and all were called to silence, wanting to hear him speak.

"We have the spear. We have each other, and we have got hope. It's time to go home!"

Cheers rang out across the deck. Song leapt down and approached Taylor.

"Well done, Colonel!" she shouted and patted him on the shoulder, but he winced in pain as a result, "I have just had reports of several small Morohta vessels lifting off the planet. They are fleeing. Do we pursue and stop them from relaying these events?"

Taylor shook his head.

"No. It's time for us all to go home. Let them get back to Bolormaa. Let them know we have killed one of her sons, and that we have the means to end her. She will now feel the fear we once felt."